Hoodfellas III

Ready to Die

By

Richard Jeanty

RJ Publications, LLC

Newark, New Jersey

The characters and events in this book are fictitious. Any resemblance to actual persons, living or dead is purely coincidental.

RJ Publications
richjeanty@yahoo.com
www.rjpublications.com
Copyright © 2011 by RJ Publications
All Rights Reserved
ISBN 0981999816
978-0981999814

Printed in Canada

April 2011

1 2 3 4 5 6 7 8 9 10

Acknowledgement

I would like to thank all the people who have supported me through my writing career for the past nine years.

To my baby girl, Rishanna, daddy loves you unconditionally and endlessly.

Special shout-out goes to my pop for his continued support.

I would especially like to thank Chanel Caraway for her devotion to this project. You know where my heart is.

Thank yous go out to all the bookclubs and readers who continue to encourage me to write and stay the course.

I would like to give a big shout- out to the street vendors, especially Pogo, Ismael, Ali, Mamadou, Henry, Emilio and my main man, Chris B, in Brooklyn. I also would like to thank and acknowledge Frugal Books in Boston as the only store that has supported me from the beginning and for continuing to do so.

Thanks to all the book retailers and distributors who make it possible for my books to stay relevant.

A special shout-out goes to all the New York book vendors and entrepreneurs. A big shout-out to my family all over the world: my cousins in Paris, Montreal, Miami, Atlanta, Haiti and everywhere in between.

If I forgot about anybody, just imagine the pressure I was under trying to finish this book, it wasn't done on purpose and I still have love for you. My head has shrunk a little, since finishing this book. It was a big load off! LOL!

Introduction

The wonderful thing about writing a story is the ability to control the direction of the story, and make it as fun or horrific as possible. This series has come to end for me, but it was pure joy writing it. While the characters I created for this story have been made up, there are far too many real examples of these characters in our own neighborhoods. It's fine to find entertainment value in these street novels that glorify the street life, but the reality is that I have never personally met any street hustler in real life who lived happily ever after.

Keeping things in perspective is the key to understanding, but too many people in our hood have lost their vision of reality. It's unfortunate that drugs, prostitution, murder and other crimes continue to devastate our community. However, it's also great that we now have an outlet to let the world know what's going on in our world.

These aren't the stories that are glorified by Hollywood for financial gain. These are the true stories of calamity that continue to be a perpetuated cycle in our community. We need to stand up and "Emancipate ourselves from mental slavery," as stated by our gifted and heroic, brother, Bob Marley, so that our children can have a better future in the hood.

Don't be fooled to think that you will make it out of the hood because of your illegal hustle. I can bet you'd find 99% of the hustlers you grew up admiring are either dead or in jail, as a result of their illegal hustle. We have to educate ourselves in order to emancipate ourselves.

Peace out!

Home Sweet Home

Deon and his crew hopped in the two helicopters that met them halfway from the Miami port. Going through customs was not an option as Rosie, Evelyne and Maribel did not have legal visas to enter the United States. Also, the bullet-riddled body of Tweak being carried across the waters would pose a threat and too many questions would have to be answered. The risk was just too high. The escorting Coast Guard vessel turned a blind eye to the helicopters that picked up the crew about ten miles away from shore. Jean Paul made sure that the bag containing the $250,000.00 pay-off was easily found when the Coast Guard boarded the cruise ship for a routine check. Surely the four National Guardsmen had never seen such a huge payday since joining the National Guard, but they still had to go through the search in case a superior figure was lurking around.

Deon and his crew took to the sky and landed at a private heliport in Miami where they were met and driven straight to a private morgue where Tweak's body would be held until his funeral the following Saturday. Laying low was the order of the day. The money had to be stashed and the basic necessities had to be gotten by the crew. Riding around town in a stretch limousine for the next week until Tweak's funeral was not an option. Transportation and lodging were essential and the pilot who flew the helicopter had the connections to make everything happen. Deon was handed the keys to a twenty thousand square-foot, twenty-bedroom and twenty five-bathroom house, located on Star Island, near Miami Beach, Florida at a cost of two-hundred thousand dollars per month. He also had access to the three vehicles parked in the three-car garage of the home. The flashiest of all was the yellow Lamborghini that belonged to the homeowner who used the house as a second home while he was away in Los Angeles shooting his next big blockbuster. The other two cars, a black S Class Mercedes and a white Range Rover were also available for the guys to use.

The home was spectacular and immaculate in its splendor. Only movie stars, athletes, rich politicians, moguls and rock stars lived on Star Island. The home forced Deon and the Hoodfellas to reconsider the reasons why they had been working so diligently to get money so they could live the fabulous life. The ladies were enamored by the charm of the house and its décor. Having gone from the slums of Haiti, the ghettos of the Dominican Republic and the trailer parks of Massachusetts, the ladies were impressed. This was the lifestyle they dreamed of; the Hoodfellas still had enough money for all of them to live that lifestyle.

South Beach

After settling in their new abode, Deon and the crew wanted to get a little taste of South Beach. The whole crew loaded up in the three cars and headed straight down to South Beach. Deon and Cindy rode in the Lamborghini while the rest of the crew rode in the Mercedes and Range Rover. All eyes were on the caravan of luxury cars as the crew rolled down Ocean Avenue. The yellow Lamborghini took the lead as the black S Class Mercedes Benz followed with Smitty behind the wheel, while Maribel sat next to him in the front seat and Rosie in the back seat. Crusher followed behind in the White Range Rover with Evelyne next to him. The crew was just out to check the scene and perhaps grab a bite to eat. Deon had also decided to drop the top on the Lamborghini so he could take in a little sun. Whispers of "sellout" were coming from all the sisters who noticed the white girl sitting in the front seat next to Deon.

Deon dismissed the hating whispers as he and Cindy continued to drive down Ocean Ave until they decided to pull up to a seafood restaurant for dinner. The keys to all three vehicles were given to the valet as the crew sat under a canopy outside to enjoy a seafood feast. Maribel was looking as gorgeous as ever when the Cuban waiter decided he wanted to talk to her in Spanish. "Hola, como esta?" he said to her. "Bien, gracias," she responded kindly. She almost felt a sense of nostalgia while speaking to the waiter in Spanish. It had been a while since she spoke her native tongue. However, when the guy started asking her why she was having dinner with a bunch a Negroes, she became obviously livid. She told the dude to buzz off. The guy wouldn't let up and Deon, Smitty and Crusher could see the obvious frustration on her face. At that point, she told Deon it would be best to request a different waiter because the guy was bothering her. Smitty was gazing at the dude as if he was ready to take him out. "What you looking at, tough guy?" the Cuban waiter said to Smitty. His long, slick looking ponytail must've given him the confidence of Samson or something. Smitty almost got up to stab him in his eye with a fork, before Deon interfered. "Not now. We're not trying to get into anything with the cops," Deon told Smitty.

The crew acted as if nothing was wrong when a new waiter was assigned to them. After ordering some of the most expensive seafood dishes on the menu, Deon ordered a bottle of wine to celebrate their voyage back from Haiti. Everyone toasted while waiting for the food. The new waiter was a young brother who obviously had it in for the Cuban waiter. "These mu'fuckin' Cubans think they run shit around here. They always got some shit to say about black people," he told the crew. "Hey man, what time does this place shut down?" Deon nonchalantly asked the waiter. "We close at 2AM," he revealed. Deon figured that most of the waiters got off around that time, so he planned on paying the fresh-mouthed Cuban waiter a visit later on. After eating, the crew left a $500.00 tip for the black waiter and hopped back in their cars to go home.

On the way home, Maribel started revealing to Smitty all the shit that the Cuban waiter was saying about black people. He told her that black people were lazy, good for nothing drug dealers and savages. Maribel took offense because her life changed drastically because of the crew. She knew what would've happened if Deon found out what the waiter had said about them. The waiter needed to be dealt with. A good asswhoop was in order.

Ocean Avenue was relatively dead around two o'clock in the morning during midweek. As the Cuban waiter made his way to his moped around an alley in the back of the restaurant, he felt a tap on his shoulder. He didn't even realize what hit him as Crusher landed a devastating blow to his right jaw, knocking him out instantly. A barrage of punches came moments later from Smitty and Crusher. The Cuban waiter was left bloodied and clinging to life in the back of the alley while the two assailants made their way back to the mansion in the black Benz that was parked a couple of blocks away. The waiter would need reconstructive surgery to put his face back together. He never recalled what happened and no report was ever filed as a result.

Ma Dukes

Tweak's mom had relocated to Florida after Tweak left the country, which worked in Deon's favor. Tweak had made it known he was a mama's boy and he made sure his mother knew his whereabouts at all times. He also told the crew to take his body to his mother if anything ever happened to him. Tweak had sent his mom enough money to buy a home, a car and to retire comfortably without having any financial worries. Tweak was always a good son, and his mother knew of his illegal dealings, not that she approved of them. A former hustler in her own right, Tweak's mom boosted for a long time in order to provide for her children. Having come from the Jamaica Plain Projects, she could barely feed her two children on the government assistance she received monthly. When she decided to get a job to supplement her income, her benefits were cut off. She soon quit her job, went back on welfare and started boosting. Jordan Marsh, Filene's and Neiman Marcus were her favorite stores. She would steal designer handbags, leather goods and expensive sweaters and sell them for pennies on the dollar in the streets. All of Tweak's friends referred to her as Ma Dukes.

Ma Dukes had established a clientele that was so tight-knit that people would call her with their orders and she was guaranteed payment before she stole anything. As her boosting skills improved, so did surveillance technology. Unaware of the camera fixated on her, one day she was at Filene's filling up an empty Filene's bag with goods when two plainclothes security officers approached and placed her under arrest for theft. Her ammo was to walk into the store carrying an empty shopping bag from the store that she brought from home, and fill it up with as much merchandise as possible while looking around for security. After that arrest, Ma Dukes was given three years probation and she vowed never to boost again, because she didn't want to be away from her children. Their daddies were not involved in their lives. When Tweak went to prison, she lost all hope of ever moving out of the projects. Tweak was the most intelligent of her three children and she knew that one day he would do something great with his life to help the rest of the family.

While Tweak was in prison, she lost another son in a street shooting at the hands of police officers. Her son was coming home from football practice one day when he and his friends got into a little squabble with a rival group of kids on the bus. One thing led to another and the police were called. Upon arrival, the police noticed the melee and attempted to take control of the situation. Unfortunately, her son was reaching for his cellphone when a bevy of bullets was unloaded into his body. The cops used the excuse that they saw 'a shiny black object' that resembled a gun to justify the shooting of a young man wearing his football practice gear. The police used her blemished record as a booster and the fact that her daughter had become a regular inmate at the police station for prostitution, to vilify the whole family. Ma Dukes' lawyers, however, sued the city and received a settlement of 1.2 million dollars for the unjustifiable shooting of her son, years later after Tweak had been released from prison. After lawyer fees and helping family members, as well as helping her daughter get off drugs, she almost squandered all of the money.

It was her lovely son who came to her rescue after his bid in prison. Tweak always wanted to care for his mother, and Deon gave him the opportunity to earn enough money to care for her. For that, she would kill anyone who crossed her son. Needless to say, Ma Dukes was devastated when she found out her son was killed in Haiti. She would have bombed the entire island of Haiti if she could after receiving that news. "Please tell me you killed the bastards who killed my son!" she said to Deon, after he told her the news. "Of course, we did, Ma Dukes. I'm sorry about what happened, but we killed every single one of them," he told her for comfort. For some odd reason, that little bit of news seemed to have brought some kind of relief to Ma Dukes. She at least knew her son went out like a soldier after Deon explained to her what happened. Deon also handed her a bag with over two million dollars that belonged to Tweak. He also told her that he would take care of all the funeral expenses. "Even though, Tweak is gone, trust and believe that you still have a son in all of us," Deon told Ma Dukes as he pointed to Crusher and Smitty. He continued, "If you ever need anything, don't hesitate to call. Crusher and I will always be there for you. You have always been like a mother to us, anyway." "Thank you, boys. I will see you at the wake on Friday. I have to start getting some of my family down here for the funeral," she told them. "Don't worry about that, Ma Dukes. Just give us the names of the people you want down here, and we'll take care of it," Deon told her. "Thank you, baby," Ma Dukes said, as tears invaded her eyes.

A week later, Deon had a lavish funeral for Tweak at one of the most prestigious funeral parlors in Miami. Family and friends gathered for the wake on Friday night where everyone came to view Tweak's body in an elaborately designed coffin. A picture of Tweak wearing a nice suit after he came home with his government name, Ernest Townsend, was placed on an easel near the coffin. Tweak's sister showed up looking clean and sober. Ma Dukes couldn't contain herself at the sight of her baby boy lying in a coffin. She was emotionally drained after losing two of her children to gunshots.

After burying Tweak's body at the cemetery the next day, Ma Dukes revealed to Deon that she had never touched the settlement money she received from the City of Boston for the shooting death of her son. She had placed the money in a special account with the hope to give it to Tweak one day to open a legitimate business. She had been taking care of friends and family with the illegal money that Tweak had been sending to her. "I want you boys to leave the streets alone," she said to Deon through sobs. Deon had never really thought about the deadly consequences of the streets, but for the first time in his life, he paused and started thinking about the grief he had caused since the death of his comrades during battle. "You know I consider you a son, and I still want you to use this money to open a legitimate business, that's the least I can offer you as a surrogate mother. I'm tired of all this death and killing going on around me," she said sadly. Ma Dukes had been a soldier herself for so long; she just couldn't take losing another person close to her. She was willing to retire her gangster for the betterment of the rest of the people around her. As vindictive as she felt her heart could be, she was more afraid of the wrath of death upon another family member or a close friend.

A New Course?

There were two reasons why Deon wanted to avenge Short Dawg and No Neck's death. The first was because he felt he owed them that much as a friend and brother, so they didn't die in vain. The second reason was because he didn't want to become a victim in case he ever ran into the people who killed No Neck and Short Dawg on the streets of Boston. Though Ma Dukes' words pierced right through his heart, Deon knew that he couldn't leave the job undone. He had to settle the score before he set on a new path in life. "Ma Dukes, I promise you that I'm gonna walk away from this the minute me and the crew get back from Boston. I have to settle this last score in the name of the streets and what we stand for as a crew," he told her. "My son, you must understand that in this game, we always have one last score to settle. It's called a last score because it always ends up being the end of the person trying to settle the score. I went to jail because I needed one last score. I can tell you about thousands of crackheads, drug dealers, thieves and risk-takers who needed to settle one last score. It's not worth it," she said. Deon didn't even want to allow Ma Dukes' words to marinate. There was no way he was going to let these bastards get away with killing his friends. He wanted revenge, even if it was the end for him.

There was no turning back from this. Deon was back in the States and he had to stake his claim to let those fools know who was king of the streets. However, Deon took heed to Ma Dukes' words and decided to set up a legitimate business in Miami before setting off for Boston.

With so many actors, rappers and other stars visiting Miami Beach on a daily basis, Deon thought it would be profitable to establish a limousine service, as well as a luxury car rental company in Miami. Everyone in South Beach seemed to be sucked in by the high life and Deon took notice right away while visiting South Beach with his crew. The frequent visits by so many stars and out of town ballers trying to make an impression on the beautiful women visiting South Beach, the business idea was a no-brainer. Deon and the crew would be legit and they could live the luxurious lifestyle they always dreamed of, legally.

Ma Dukes' money from the lawsuit was more than enough for Deon to use as start-up capital to secure a five million dollar loan for his business. Of course, he replaced every dime she gave him from his stash that he brought back from Haiti. Ma Dukes' name was on all the papers as one of the majority owners of the business, while Deon and his crew's names were listed as investors into The Luxurious Life, LLC. Under that umbrella, Deon planned to expand his business into more than just a limousine and luxury car company. He wanted to offer those people who could afford it, every luxury under the sun, such as private planes, yachts, private concerts with celebrity artists, special trips to exotic locations around the world, personal chefs, trainers, personal stylists, personal shoppers and even private beautiful escorts, etc. His dream was to design a one-stop shop for those people seeking luxury for anything in life, as long as they could afford it.

Within a couple of weeks, a beautiful, luxurious office suite was rented on Collins Avenue. The office offered a conference room, a reception area, four private offices, an underground parking lot big enough to accommodate twenty limousines and a fleet of one hundred cars. There was also a section of the lot that was used as a car wash to keep the limousines and the luxury vehicles clean on a daily basis. A well-lit sign with the company's name and logo hung above the building, while a Lamborghini and a Ferrari were parked in the front to attract the customers. Deon hired some of the best lawyers in South

Florida to ensure the proper licensing and paperwork for his business. Everyone from his crew had a position in the company, but he also hired the former general manager of Hertz from the South Florida branch to run his company. Deon knew nothing about car rentals, contracts, insurance and everything else related to the business. He wanted to learn from the best, so he hired the best, and paid him the best salary in the business.

A fleet of limousines was bought from a company that specialized in limousine deliveries. The company offered everything from stretched Hummers and Range Rover Limousines to your basic black Lincoln Towncar limousines. There wasn't a luxury brand that was not available from the company. It was the same with the luxury cars. Deon purchased Bentleys, Rolls Royces, Mercedes Benzes, Maybachs, BMW's, Audis, Aston Martins, Range Rovers, Jaguars, and every other luxury brand in both convertible and hard top. If a customer had the money to spend, he wanted to make sure he had the car to offer to them. Deon wanted the company to be first class and the first of its kind in South Beach. A representative was hired to focus on establishing relationships with high end hotels, like the Delano, Ritz Carlton and a few others on South Beach to help accommodate the guests. Special discount rates were offered in order for the company to compete with other existing companies vying for a business relationship with the luxury hotels.

It took a couple of months for the company to get off the ground, but with a radio, television and internet campaign, and a celebrity face from the Miami Heat to represent the company, The Luxurious Life, LLC started gaining ground in no time. No expenses were spared to make the company successful. The business manager, Jason Grant used his influence in South Florida to gain access to rappers, singers, actors and athletes to make sure the company received notoriety at all of South Beach's biggest events. There were times when celebrities were offered a free pick-up from the airport to special events. Luxurious Life limousines were present at all red-carpet events in Miami. The brand was becoming synonymous with the high life and celebrities. Deon and his crew worked hard for almost a year to make sure the business thrived. After learning every operational aspect of the business, everything was like clockwork. It was then that Deon felt comfortable enough to be away from the business for a few days so he could take care of his unfinished business in Boston.

Rekindling Old Friendships

Deon left the crew behind and flew to Boston, along with Smitty. By then, there was no need to get on a commercial flight. He wanted to fly under the radar. He hired a private jet for all his personal trips and he conducted business while up in the air. For the most part, Deon had tried his best to avoid going to Boston until he was ready. It had been a while since he visited Boston, but he knew exactly where to go to get reconnected to the people he needed. It was nostalgic for him to drive down Blue Hill Avenue in a chauffeur driven limousine to see the dilapidated streets that he once ran. The darkly tinted windows of the limousine shielded him and Smitty from any possible enemies.

His first order of business was to go down to Chinatown to visit an old friend that he met in prison who had assisted him in the past with a big job. Tommy Li had been out of prison just as long as Deon and he wasn't the type of man who sat around waiting for a handout. Just like Deon, Tommy Li had been building his empire in

Chinatown and was now the boss of the New Chinese Connection he started. After entering the building wearing a dark-colored Armani suit and smelling like a million bucks, Deon was greeted by a beautiful Asian woman that could grace the cover of any of those popular fashion magazines such as Elle and Glamour; tall, slender and so sexy that a man could get lost in her eyes alone, but she was also deadly. "Can I help you?" she asked Deon. "Yes beautiful, I'm here to see Tommy. He's expecting me," Deon told her. "I need to pat you down before you're allowed to enter the building. Deon took offense because he hadn't been patted down since he left prison, and as a businessman he had left that kind of treatment in his past. "I really don't think that's necessary," he told her. "I'm not asking you what you think, you're either going to get a pat down or you're not getting beyond the reception area," she said. "Who's gonna stop me, you?" Deon said while laughing. As Deon tried to step forward past the Asian beauty, he didn't even realize how she got him down to the ground on his stomach while his hands were pushed up towards his head in pain.

It was then that Tommy emerged in the reception area and said, "Deon, I see you've met my beautiful bodyguard, Rachel Ming." She still hadn't let go of his arm. "She's breaking my arm, man," Deon said while breathing heavily. Tommy signaled for her to let go of him. As Deon got up, he balled his fist as if he was about to hit her, but she didn't even flinch. "I see you're still in the business of inflicting pain, but how can a woman so beautiful be so rough?" he asked Tommy. "Deception is the name of game. If you can't fool people, you won't survive in my business. Let's go to my office so we can talk," Tommy suggested. Tommy went back to his office and pulled out a bag of money that Deon had given to him years ago before he went to Haiti. "What's this?" Deon asked as Tommy handed the bag over to him. "It's the money you left with us to take care of the people who killed Short Dawg and No Neck. The job was never done 'cause I never heard back from you, so there's no reason to accept the money," Tommy told him. "You mean you held on to the money this whole time?" Deon asked perplexed. "I'm a man of my word. We didn't know where to find the killers because we had no idea what crew they came from," Tommy told him. "I was hoping to pick up their skulls as a memento. But that's no problem, you're still gonna do the job, right?" Deon asked with curiosity. "Is there still a couple of million dollars in that bag?" Tommy asked while laughing. "My man," Deon said while moving in to give Tommy dap. "Well, all I know about them was that they were called The Clean-up Crew and they were from Orchard Park Projects," Deon revealed.

"You know I have since moved up the ranks in my organization, so I won't be directly involved with this, but I'm gonna make sure we get it done for you," Tommy assured him. "The name of the guy whose head I want you to bring me is Case. He was Short Dawg's friend who betrayed him," Deon told him. "There's an added bonus for the head, an extra two million dollars." "Consider it done. I'll put some of my best men on it as soon as possible. It's always nice doing business with you. I didn't offer you anything to drink because I know you're not a drinker. Take care, my friend. We'll be in touch soon," Tommy said before the two departed.

As Deon walked by Rachel Ming, he acted like he was gonna hit her again, but she still didn't flinch. "You're a tough chick, but don't be going around thinking that you can whoop a man's ass. I'ma have to shoot you next time," he said while holding in his laugh.

Meanwhile, Smitty was waiting in the limousine impatiently. Unfortunately, while he was sitting there waiting for Deon, a young man decided it was advantageous to act like he was trying to get some spare change and found himself knocked out with a bottle of Grey Goose cracked over his head. "Your friend is crazy," the driver said as he opened the door to let Deon into the limousine. The man was on the ground noticeably bleeding next to the limousine. "What happened here?" Deon asked. "This fool had me pull down my window and acted like he was looking for some spare change. When I handed him a twenty dollar bill because I thought he looked hungry, he reached out and tried to snatch my chain. I introduced his head to the bottle of Grey Goose and he's been out since," Smitty told him. "Let's get outta here," Deon told the driver. "I can't even leave you in the limo for five minutes without you doing some damage to somebody?" Deon said while shaking his head at the situation. "It wasn't my fault, man. He was trying to snatch my chain off my neck. I had to do something," Smitty pleaded. To his credit, the driver never got a chance to see the man trying to snatch Smitty's chain. He only heard the crack of the bottle against the man's head.

Old Territory

While Deon was out of prison trying to build an empire that would financially set him and his crew for life, his mother got early parole and was let out of prison in his absence. Unfortunately, Deon didn't discover the news until his trip to Boston. He had been a rich man for the last few years while his mother struggled to make ends meet. She desperately tried to locate him, but no one knew his whereabouts. It was now December and Christmas was fast approaching. Serena Bender could hardly keep her lights on, as her gas had already been turned off. She used an electric blanket to keep warm at night, and even that would soon be removed from her grip, as her electric bill had been delinquent for the last four months and termination notices of her electric service arrived in her mailbox almost on a daily basis.

Serena barely had enough skills to obtain a job that could financially sustain her in the third most expensive city in America, Boston. Her measly minimum wage job at McDonald's barely kept a roof over her head. The rundown one-bedroom apartment she rented in a dilapidated section of Roxbury was roach and mice infested, but it was better than life behind bars for Serena. She braced the cold everyday to walk to her job, as she couldn't afford the bus fare to and from work. On the coldest days, Serena sacrificed a day's meal in order to travel on the bus to work. While McDonald's threw away food at the end of the night, one of their employees was hungry most of the time. No policy was ever put in place at her job where the left-over food could be obtained by employees. Fearing another stint in prison, Serena chose to be a law-abiding citizen by refusing to offer herself a "five finger" discount from the food or the register. Life was hard for Serena. She had come a long way from being the young, beautiful and fabulous woman she once was. With a deformed face and barely any self-esteem left, she chose to be a loner.

Fortunately, Deon still had friends in the old neighborhood that he sought to help because of the upcoming holidays. The old man who offered him free haircuts when he was a young boy roaming the neighborhood was still at the same place, though the shop could barely stay open. Nothing about the old barbershop changed, except for the old man himself. Forced to continue to work past his retirement age, the old man went to the shop everyday, even if to shoot the breeze with the other younger barbers, who by then claimed all the new customers. The old man was happy to see an older Deon walk through his shop wearing an Armani suit and looking like he was a billionaire. "Deon!" the old man exclaimed without hesitation as Deon set foot inside the shop. Deon was shocked that the old man even remembered who he was. He hadn't been at that barbershop since he was seventeen years old, before he went to prison. "Mr. Lawson, you still remember who I am?" Deon asked surprised. "Boy, I was cutting your hair since you were a baby, I would never forget a customer that I watched grow up in front of me," he said. Very few people knew that Deon had gotten out of prison and came home a few years back, but everybody knew when he went to prison at seventeen years old. "Did you just get out?" the old man asked. "No, Mr. Lawson. I've been out. Been doing some things and I came back to check out the old neighborhood," he said. "Well, you look damn good doing it," Mr. Lawson said while smiling. Deon could tell that Mr. Lawson was proud of him.

Meanwhile all the young barbers in the shop were wondering who the mysterious, charming man was. Deon was not the type of guy to make a loud entrance or announce everything about himself. He was trying to keep his voice as low as possible while talking to Mr. Lawson. Deon was also taking inventory of the old man's shop. Nothing had been renovated in the shop. The sign in front of the shop was barely hanging on with a rope tied around it to keep it from falling on somebody's head. The place looked like it was struggling. "What you been doing with yourself?" Mr. Lawson asked proudly. "Got a little business started down south, trying to get my piece of the pie," Deon told him. "Well, you look like you're doing it, son. You look like a million bucks. Have you been over there to see your mother?" Mr. Lawson asked. Deon was shocked! He thought his mother was still in prison. He hadn't planned on going to the prison to see her because he didn't want the authorities to catch up to him in case they were looking. "No, I haven't seen my mother yet," he whispered in Mr. Lawson's ear. The old man took notice right away and realized that it wasn't a subject that Deon wanted to discuss in front of the other barbers. The barbershop was barely big enough for the barbers and the customers, so there was really no room for a private conversation, but Mr. Lawson found a way. "Why don't I grab my coat, we can step outside to have a few words," he suggested. Mr. Lawson grabbed his coat off the rack and stepped out to the waiting limousine with Deon. He was all smiles when he saw the limousine outside in front of his shop. Deon quickly introduced Smitty to the old man after entering the limo.

Mr. Lawson was a little apprehensive about talking in front of Smitty once inside the limousine, but Deon nodded his head and told him that it was okay. "Well, you know Serena has been out for a few years now. She received early parole because she was a good inmate, but things ain't been so good for her since she came home. She been struggling," the old man revealed. Deon shook his head in sadness at the thought of his mom struggling to survive. "I think she would be happy to see you," Mr. Lawson said. "Do you know where I can find her?" Deon asked. "As a matter of fact, I can take you to her. She should be working at her job right now. Let me just go in there and tell the guys that I'm gonna make a run with you and that I'll be right back," he said before exiting the limousine.   An emotional feeling came over Deon at the thought of seeing his mother after over twenty years. He didn't know what to expect, but he was excited at the prospect of rescuing his mother.

Mr. Lawson came back to the limousine moments later, and directed the driver to drive down to Warren Street at the Washington Mall, where McDonald's was located. "May I please take your order?" Serena's crackling voice said over the PA system. Even though he hadn't heard his mother's voice in years, Deon recognized the familiar tone instantly. "Sure, I would like a hug, a kiss and you to go," Deon said while trying to contain himself. At first, the PA system seemed like it was playing tricks on Serena, but just like any mother, she also recognized her son's voice and the crackling of her voice came back over the PA system and asked "Deon?" seemingly in tears. "Come outside, mama," the emotional Deon said back to her. Serena dropped everything she was doing to run outside to go see her son. She had no idea that he was riding in a limousine. By the time she turned the corner of the McDonald's, Deon was standing there with two dozen roses, his arms wide open, inviting her in for a hug. He had stopped by the florist on Walk Hill to get the roses on the way to see his mom. It was a tearful moment for the two of them. It was the first time that hard ass Smitty had ever seen his boss shed a tear. Even Smitty was on the brink of shedding tears at the memory of his own mother's passing. Serena almost didn't want to let go of her son. She touched his face, kissed him and hugged him while a stream of tears ran down her cheeks.

Meanwhile, Serena's boss came chasing after her when he noticed the emotional scene taking place through the window of the restaurant. He had somewhat of an idea that it could've been a reunion in the making, but he wasn't sure because Serena didn't talk much to the people at work. However, after witnessing the emotional embrace exchange, he offered to give Serena the rest of the day off. "Man, I appreciate your offer to her, but today's gonna be her last day at this job, bro," Deon said to the store manager. "Deon, I can't just leave my job because you showed up in my life. How am I gonna take care of myself, I got bills, you know?" she told him with curiosity. "You ain't gotta worry about working no more, Mama. You're coming down to Florida with me. As a matter of fact, we're going to your house now, so you can pick up only the most valuable things to you. Leave your clothes, bed and everything else behind," he told her. Serena couldn't believe that her prince charming, her son, had come back to rescue her. From the looks of things, she believed every word he said to her.

After getting inside the limousine, Serena couldn't thank Mr. Lawson enough for bringing Deon to her job. Though Serena didn't steal for herself at work, she would always hook up Mr. Lawson with an extra burger or larger drink whenever he stopped by the McDonald's where she worked. Deon introduced Smitty to his mother as the little brother he never had. The joy from their reconnection soon vanished after Deon discovered the conditions that his mother was living in. He couldn't believe his eyes when he went up to her apartment to help her gather a few of her belongings. His heart ached and he was upset with himself for not having come after her sooner. He asked her to change into the best possible clothes that she had. The best things that she could come up with were a shirt she bought from Goodwill and a pair of jeans from a thrift shop. It was good enough to get her out of town as Deon had planned to take her shopping once they made it down to Miami. The only things that Serena took with her were the sentimental pictures of Deon and her when he was a little boy. When she dated Wally, he took plenty of pictures of her wearing her fur coat while little Deon sported the latest gear in high fashion. She kept all those pictures in a shoebox as mementos. However, Deon insisted on cutting out Wally in every picture that he was in. It was a face that he never wanted to see again.

After wrapping up at Serena's apartment, Deon decided to bring Mr. Lawson back to his shop and thanked him for all that he had done to help reconnect him to his mother. He also knew that words about him being in Boston would spread very quickly by the other guys in the barbershop, and it was a matter of time before they figured out who he was. He dropped Mr. Lawson off and handed him twenty thousand dollars in hundred dollar bills. Mr. Lawson couldn't pray for a better holiday season. From there, Deon went straight to the airport where a private jet was waiting for him, his mom and Smitty. "D, are we heading back already?" Smitty asked disappointed. "Yeah, we gotta bounce because too many people saw me already," Deon told him. "Damn, man, I didn't even get a chance to enjoy Boston," he said frustrated. "You don't be out there in Boston like that, anyway. You're part of a highly sought-after crew, remember that," Deon reiterated. Deon threw away the dingy jacket his mother was wearing before they boarded the plane. Serena couldn't believe her eyes. Her son had come a long way and made good in life. She was very proud of him. "I don't care how you got this money, or what you're doing to get it, but whatever you're doing, do it to the best of your abilities. Don't ever let anybody take anything away from you. Don't worry about what anybody thinks of you. You must be ready to die for yours," his mother bestowed upon him before the plane took off. Deon pondered his mother's words for a minute before realizing what she said came from a fighting place. She didn't fight hard enough when she had the chance, so now she wanted her son to fight for everything that he had. He just smiled at his mother before dosing off to sleep on the plane.

Miami

The minute the plane landed, Deon knew exactly what his first order was going to be. After gathering his suitcase, Deon threw everything in the waiting limo and told the driver to drive straight to the Aventura Mall to take his mother shopping. The driver pulled up to the entrance by Nordstrom, Deon handed his mother twenty-five thousand dollars in cash and told her to spend it on any clothing item she wanted. Deon decided to stay in the limousine while Smitty and the driver went in with his mother to help with her bags. He had a few business phone calls to make while his mother shopped. His once upon at time, stylish mother, knew exactly what she was going to buy. Though the new clothes would boost her self-esteem, she still had to look at herself in the mirror and deal with her deformed faced on a daily basis.

While Serena was shopping away, Deon was making arrangements for another surprise for his mother. He got in touch with a few associates he knew in Miami that led him to do the most admiring thing that he could offer his mom to help change her outlook on life. Deon also checked to see what was going on with his business and the next step to improve the brand. Meanwhile, Serena couldn't help splurging on everything from jewelry, to clothing and perfume. By the time she was done, Smitty and the limo driver could barely carry all the bags of items she bought. Serena had never been so happy, but that was just the tip of the iceberg.

Though Deon was happy to reconnect with his mother, he was still bothered by the way she looked. His memory of his mother was that of a vibrant, gorgeous woman who could land any man she wanted. He wanted to bring back the old Serena, the woman who once made men squirm at the sight of her. Deon ordered the driver to drive directly to Palm Beach to the office of a highly recommended plastic surgeon. However, he only gave the driver the address without mentioning it was a doctor's office. On the ride to the surgeon's office, Deon kept staring at one of the pictures of him and his mother and how beautiful she looked standing in front of her BMW rocking a fur coat, while holding his hand. He smiled at the thought of his beautiful, youthful mother and the memories that he had of her at that time.

Deon was a proud man who wanted the world to see the best of him at all times. There was no doubt that having his mother in his presence was the best thing that had happened to him in a long time, but he didn't want to introduce her to his friends with her face looking deranged. He had to convince the doctor to perform emergency cosmetic surgery and to also keep her under his care until she recovered completely in a luxury suite near the doctor's office. No price was too big and Deon didn't even hesitate when the doctor quoted him a price of one hundred and fifty thousand dollars to bring back her old look. Certified as one of the best cosmetic surgeons in the country, Deon entrusted the life of his mother in the doctor's hands. The most attractive term for the doctor was the fact that the money would be paid to him in cash, something he could keep from the IRS while continuing to live a lavish lifestyle.

Serena agreed to Deon's terms to be blindfolded on the way to the doctor's office. He wanted his mother to gain back her confidence the next time she looked in the mirror. When they arrived at the doctor's office, she was asked a series of questions about allergies and other symptoms that could prevent the operation. After running a few tests, the doctor determined that Serena was cleared to go under the knife to have this life-changing operation. Deon left the picture with the doctor and warned him that he didn't want her to look a bit different from it after recovery. The operation was successful and Deon hired a couple of full-time nurses to care for his mother around the clock until she fully recovered. When she went to the doctor three weeks later to take the bandages off, all Serena could do was cry. She couldn't believe her eyes when she looked in the mirror. It was as if God himself had performed a miracle on her. Serena's face was so nice and tight, she looked like she could be Deon's sister, though age appropriate. She regained her confidence and in no time she was back to her old hustling self, but this time she was running things for a big company that her son owned.

Mistress of the House

The transition and reconnection of Serena and Deon went smoothly. For the first time in Deon's life, he had someone in his corner who loved him unconditionally and she was down with him to the death. After purchasing the mansion that he initially rented when he first moved to Miami with the crew, Deon wanted to make it clear to them that they were all free to do what they wanted to do, including being part of the empire he was trying to build. There was plenty of money to go around and everyone could be set for life if each of them took his/her share of the money. That deal was always on the table and Deon was serious about that. However, the crew chose to stay a part of The Luxurious Life, LLC. The new girls had no vested interest in the company, but Deon decided to give them a share anyway.

Crusher was the only original member left of the crew who had served time with Deon in prison. The other fallen soldiers were honored through foundations set up in their names and financial assistance given to their close surviving family members. Smitty, the unofficial adopted son of the crew, carved a bigger stake for himself after the gun battle in Haiti. Though not the brightest man, Crusher was very ambitious and he believed in Deon's ability. He had a choice to take his share of almost fifteen million dollars with him to start a new life, but he chose to invest most of it in the company. Crusher was a simple man who didn't care much about luxury or the fabulous life. He bought a ranch a few miles out of the city where he planned on settling after he helped Deon solidify the company. His money would be multiplied ten times over if things went according to Deon's plan. So far, there was no reason to worry and all that was promised to him was legally binding on paper. Deon was a man of his word, and Crusher trusted him with his life. The only luxury Crusher bought himself was a monster truck that he always dreamed about when he was a kid. Outfitted with the loudest and best sound system, the shiniest wheels, custom made interior and a super-charged engine, Crusher's Ford Expedition was like no other.

Crusher's thirst for the wild life was also taking a new direction. He no longer yearned to be with Evelyne and Rosie at the same time. He was a little more fond of Evelyne and she was head over heels for him. She was mesmerized by the big bear. Rosie could do without the romance. She was more excited about the lifestyle and the wild sex that they were having. She was never intent on taking Crusher seriously. In addition, Rosie was more like a bird who needed her freedom to fly wherever she wanted. Crusher and Evelyne became an item and he was looking to build a future with her. Their ideals were pretty much the same and he wanted nothing more than to be exclusively with her.

The mansion had become the Hoodfellas' compound for the most part. The twenty thousand square-foot home was so big, everyone had a wing. When Serena moved into the in-law suite, outfitted with a master bedroom, bathroom, a living room and a bar, she was happy with her new abode. She also became the mistress of the house. She was the mother to everybody and made sure everybody was fine. While in prison, Serena had also become a pretty decent cook. Though Deon had enough money to hire three chefs to cater to the culinary needs of his crew, he really enjoyed his mom's home cooking. Serena came into Deon's life when he was becoming a legitimate businessman. She felt she no longer had to worry about his safety and that her baby was on the right path in life. However, the course to Deon's new path would not be so smooth when the Italian mob decided to stake their claim in his business.

Serena was not the same street smart hustler who had gone to prison many years ago. She had become a hardened criminal with the wit and smarts of a professional convict and a strong heart to defend those closest to her. She wouldn't lay down her guns to surrender. A blaze of glory was more the ammo she would follow at this point in her life, but she hoped that it would never come to that. This time Serena was willing to die for her son.

Trouble Brewing

The Luxurious Life, LLC was doing very well. Deon had secured enough business in South Beach for his business to turn a high profit within the first year of operation. While Deon was watching his company's moves and growth, somebody else was watching his pockets. Unaware of the history of the company and the people behind it, the mob set out to test the waters with the Hoodfellas.

First, it was the casual introduction of the two muscle men who were soldiers in the mob and the Capo walking into Deon's office for a meeting to demand a share of his business. As a former gangster of a different kind, Deon understood the rules of the game. He almost wanted to pull out his gun and blast the heads off the three gangsters in his office, but he decided to hear them out. His right hand men were standing behind them with their fingers on the trigger. Sweat beads formed on the brow of the over-hyped youngster, Smitty, as anger took over his emotions while he stood behind Deon to listen to these goons trying to extort money from them. Smitty was always action-prone and those men had better be careful of what they said in his presence. The muscle-bound, Crusher, was a little calmer, but nonetheless, just as dangerous. His "In Gun We Trust" motto was something that he lived by, and carrying more than two at a time was not unusual. The Capo and his men weren't too impressed, though. They didn't think there was enough muscle in that company to stand against them.

Evelyne, Rosie, Cindy and Maribel looked like typical professional women in their business attire, conducting business for the company. However, hiding behind the supply closet was a stash of machine guns and enough ammunition to blast these mob guys from Miami to Las Vegas. The mob never saw beyond their feminine attire and duties in the office. "Well, this is our town and businesses here are run through us," said the Capo to Deon. "I had no idea you guys were part of City Hall," Deon said sarcastically while cracking a smile. "We have a wise guy here, hey?" said the Capo in frustration. "I think you've said enough Mr… what was your name again?" Deon asked in a more sarcastic tone. "I'm Mr. Russo, to you," the Capo said with authority. "Well, Mr. Russo, I think our meeting is over. Have a good day," Deon said as Crusher and Smitty raised their guns to enforce Mr. Russo's exit. "You have one week to consider our deal. I'll be in touch," Russo said before heading out the door. One of the big Italian muscle heads considered throwing his weight around before he left, but when he noticed how an angry Crusher grabbed the stapler from Deon's desk and easily broke it in half with one hand; he quickly reconsidered and exited with his boss.

Deon knew that trouble was coming his way and there was no way he was going to meet the demands of the mob. They were trying to squeeze fifty thousand dollars out of him a week. Something had to be done, and it had to be done fast. Deon had to gather the crew to figure out how they were going to proceed against the mob, something he never anticipated.

The ironic thing was that it was only a few years ago that Deon was doing the twisting of the arms back in the hood, but he had reasons for doing it. Now it was his turn to get his arms twisted and he didn't plan on going out like a sucker. Though Crusher had started to mellow out a little as he matured, he would never back down from a fight. It was in his blood to be a fighter and to protect what was his. The Hoodfellas had come a long way to earn everything they had while losing a few soldiers in the war on their way to the top. There was no way they were going to roll over and allow the mob to intimidate them. Deon also knew that he needed a lot more muscle in order to go up against the mob. His crew was featherweight compared to the mob, and his fire power was nowhere near as strong.

The Mob

First, Deon had to figure out the make-up of the Borgata, which was the basic structure of the mob society. He also had to learn about his enemy and the family he was going up against or he was doomed for failure. Failure had never been an option in Deon's life. He was born to win.

The Mancini Borgata was an old family of mobsters that had risen to power after the fall of the previous mob boss who was busted by the FBI when an Italian agent was able to infiltrate his organization from the roots. Most of the members of the Giordano family were taken down after ruling South Florida with an iron fist for over twenty-five years. The Mancini Borgata settled for the northern part of Miami, because they had no choice. However, after the Giordano Borgata was dissipated by the bust, the Mancini Borgata saw it as an opportunity to take over the southern part of Florida as well. The Mancini family was in position for the takeover only because the FBI had done a great job busting most of the members of the Giordano Borgata and forcing the judge to hand out sentences in bundles of twenty-five to life to most of the Giordano Borgata members. The Mancini Borgata has been violently running things in South Florida since their reign.

It was rumored to be the largest mob organization ever in South Florida. The FBI has had a hard time infiltrating this organization because every member of that organization has had to prove himself in order to become a part of it. Every single member of that organization has had to commit murder in the presence of other members in order to become a part of it. All members of the Mancini Borgata have to be one hundred percent Italians. Everyone from the Capofamiglia(Don), to the Uomini Donore (Men of Honor) had to be Italian. Their hierarchy consisted of a Capofagmilia, Sotto Capo (Underboss), Consigliere (Counselor/Advisor) who was a practicing attorney, Capodecina (Group Boss/Capo) like Mr. Russo, Uomini D'onore (Men of Honor), Capo regimes (Associates, Soldiers and Family Messengers/Street Boss).

The structure of the Mancini Cosa Nostra went as followed:

The head of the family, the Godfather, or the Don was the reigning dictator named Salvatore Mancini, sometimes called The Boss. The Boss received a cut of every operation taken on by every member of his family.

Mr. Mancini was voted as boss by the Capo regimes of the family. Soon after he was voted in as the Don after the former Don succumbed to a gunshot during a gun battle with his underboss, he named his son, Francesco Mancini, the underboss. Francesco was in charge of all the Capos and in the event of Salvatore's death he was in line to become boss.

Giancarlo Rizzo served as Consigliere to the family. He was a low-profile trusted gangster who grew up with Francesco, but went on to attend law school at the University of Miami. His primary role was to play mediator of disputes or be a representative in meetings with the Giordano family. He kept the Mancini family looking as legitimate as he possibly could, but was himself, legitimate apart from some minor illegal involvement with professional athletes in the sports entertainment industry. He became the Consigliere to the family only because he went to school with Francesco and he never hid his envy for the gangster life and his admiration for gangsters. Being Italian also worked to his advantage. Though Mr. Rizzo never had his own entourage, he was still powerful within the Family. He also wielded great political power as the liaison between the Don and the important 'bought' politicians and judges at City Hall.

Giuseppe Russo was the official Capo of the family. He was in charge of the crews. There were eight different crews in the family. Each crew consisted of ten soldiers. Mr. Russo ran his own small army, but he had to follow the limitations and guidelines created by The Boss, as well as pay him his cut of his profits. Russo, a childhood friend of Francesco was nominated by him to be the Capo because of his callous actions and toughness while they were growing up. Usually, the Capos are chosen by The Boss himself, but in this case, an exception was made. Most of the soldiers who worked under Mr. Russo were associates before they became soldiers. The soldiers consisted primarily of men who grew up in the neighborhood with Francesco and Giuseppe with aspirations to become gangsters, as well as other recruited Italian ex-cons who wanted to be down with the mob.

A General's Comeback

Not long after the visit from the mob, Deon was shocked when he received a letter from Mr. Lawson that was forwarded from Mean T, fresh out of prison. Mr. Lawson remained the bridge between Deon and all the old guys from the neighborhood. Mr. Lawson had watched three different generations of young people grow up in front of him, and they all knew where to go to get connected with people from the neighborhood. Mr. Lawson was the most important public information officer for the hood. He had never sold anybody to the cops. His main job was to look out for the young people in the neighborhood and to set them straight. Always the mentor to many of the young men who grew up without a father in the Dorchester and Mattapan area, Mr. Lawson encouraged everybody to do right. His words sometimes fell on deaf ears, as was the case with Mean T and Sticky Fingers before they got embroiled in that criminal case that sent Mean T to prison for thirty years and Stick Fingers to his grave.

Mr. Lawson was a forgiving man, and he genuinely cared about Meant T as a derailed young man who had to learn life's lesson the hard way. Since visiting Mr. Lawson in Boston, Deon continued to send twenty five hundred dollars to him monthly, so he could retire in peace. Deon understood that Mr. Lawson may not have gotten to him as a young man, but he knew that he made positive changes in the lives of many other young men. It was his way of helping the old man for his good work in the hood. Mean T, however, was a tough case for Mr. Lawson from the very beginning. Raised by a single mother struggling to make ends meet, Meant T found solace and adrenaline in petty crimes. Mr. Lawson had been paying attention to the young man from the time he turned six years old. Mean T's mom would bring her son to the barbershop every three weeks on Mondays for his regular free haircuts provided by Mr. Lawson. While most barbershops closed at least two days a week, Lawson decided to offer free and discounted haircuts to the struggling, single mothers in the community every Monday, and Mean T's mom took advantage of it. Since most barbershops closed on Mondays because of the slow pace of business, Mr. Lawson figured he could use that day to give back to his community. He had become the surrogate father to many of the young men who sat in his chair for a haircut, including Mean T, Sticky Fingers (Deon's dad) and young Deon. Mr. Lawson also took the opportunity to talk to these young men while they were sitting in his chair. However, he quickly noticed the unbecoming behavior from Mean T very early on. There was always rage coming from the young man, and he had a hard time expressing himself.

Mr. Lawson made the suggestion to Ms. Gonsalves, Mean T's mother, to take him to see a doctor for evaluation, but she refused to believe that anything was wrong with her son. She wanted to prove so much to his father that she could raise him by herself; that she ended up neglecting her son psychologically. It wasn't until after Mean T got to prison that he was diagnosed with Attention Deficit Disorder. After a few scuffles with other inmates and guards at the prison, he was placed on meds, and those meds helped him cope with life behind bars when he chose to take them. Mrs. Gonsalves didn't want people to think that her son was deficient or handicapped in any way, so she chose not to follow through with Mr. Lawson's advice. The incident that sent Mean T to prison for thirty years was no surprise to Mr. Lawson. He knew deep inside that it would have led down that road some day, and there was nothing he could do about it.

After Mean T's release from prison, he tried his hardest to find a way to reconnect with some folks from his past, but many of them had moved on. His mother passed while he was in prison, due to an ailing heart. Mean T took it especially hard because she was the only family that he ever knew. His extended family always believed that he was too much of a troublemaker to be around them. He and his mother were very close, as a result. The neighborhoods had changed drastically, but one constant remained, Mr. Lawson's barbershop. It was there that he was able to connect with someone from his past. Mr. Lawson was a little hesitant at first when Mean T showed up at his barbershop. He didn't know whether or not the young man had been cured of the illness that sent him behind bars for so many years. Mean T was surprised that the old man recognized him instantly. "Tony! When did you get out?" Mr. Lawson asked as he moved to hug the husky man with a slightly gray beard and bulging biceps. "You still remember me, Mr. Lawson?" Mean T said in a shy almost childlike voice. "I was cutting your hair since you were born, why would I for get you?" Mr. Lawson told him. Mean T almost didn't want to let go of Mr. Lawson. It was the first hug that he had gotten from someone that he knew as a child. He also hadn't been called Tony since his mother passed. It was refreshing that someone remembered his name, but he didn't hesitate to let Mr. Lawson know that his name had changed from Tony to Abdul Mustafa Muhammad, due to his conversion to Islam in prison. "I see you're a Muslim now. I guess that's a good thing, right?" Mr. Lawson asked with curiosity. "Yes, Mr. Lawson. I couldn't survive all these years in prison without the blessings of Allah," Mean T told him. "I have to get used to calling you Abdul because I knew you as Tony. So don't mind me if I slip up sometimes. You know I'm getting old and the memory is not as sharp as it used to be," Mr. Lawson told him with a chuckle.

Mean T was looking around the barbershop and noticed that nothing much had changed; he was now in his late forties and came home to nobody and nothing. He used the little money that the government gave him to pay for a room in a boarding house in Roxbury. Mean T was interested in getting work, and Mr. Lawson could see the desperation in his eyes. "You were up at Walpole, right?" Mr. Lawson asked as if he wasn't sure. "Yeah, I did my whole bid up there," Abdul AKA Mean T, AKA Tony, confirmed. "So you knew Sticky Fingers' kid, I mean Deon's kid, Junior?" Mr. Lawson asked. "Yes sir. I'm the one who helped him adjust when he first got in. He was like a son to me in prison," Abdul revealed. "Is that right?" Mr.

Lawson said while shaking his head. "Well, I hear he's doing pretty good. Why don't you write him a letter explaining your situation and I'll see if I can get it to him for you. He might be able to help you out," Mr. Lawson suggested. Abdul was looking for any kind of light that could shine down his dark tunnel. He was a little more hopeful after he left Mr. Lawson's barbershop. He promised to bring the letter to Mr. Lawson the following day.

The next morning Tony was in front of Mr. Lawson's shop very early, waiting for him to open the door. That gesture alone was enough to convince Mr. Lawson that Tony was a changed man and a man of his words. After Mean T left, Mr. Lawson got on the phone to call Deon to tell him about the visit from Tony. At first, Deon had a hard time recalling who Tony was because he was so used to calling him Mean T in prison. The conversion to Islam took place years later in Tony's life. "I think he goes by the name Abdul something Muhammad now," Mr. Lawson told Deon. Right away the dots connected. "Oh, you must be talking about Mean T," Deon revealed. "You all got so many names on the street, I can't even keep up with y'all. Even rappers can't stick to one name. Jay Z don't know if he wants to be Jigga, Hov and whatever else he feels like calling himself these days. I have to listen to their music all the time in my shop because of the young barbers working here. One minute I'm hearing Hov, the other I'm hearing Jigga. Schizophrenic is what he is," Mr. Lawson said with an almost serious tone. Deon busted out laughing, but he was happy to hear that Mean T was out of prison. Mr. Lawson described him for confirmation. After hearing about the situation with Mean T, Mr. Lawson proceeded to read Tony's letter to Deon over the phone. Mean T didn't ask for any handout in his letter; he simply stated his position as a free man looking for work and that any consideration would be appreciated. Deon knew that he owed his life to Mean T and the least that he could do was to bring him to Miami to be part of his organization. "Mr. Lawson, can you please mail that letter to me? I'd appreciate it. I'm also gonna need you to get in touch with Tony. As soon as you get in touch with him, give me a call. Thanks Mr. Lawson. I appreciate the call," Deon said. "No problem. You know I'm here any time you need me. Take care of yourself, son," Mr. Lawson said before hanging up the phone.

Since Tony didn't have a phone, Mr. Lawson had to drive down to his residence to find him. It was early evening when Mr. Lawson drove down to Roxbury to find Tony. He was in his room lying on the single bed reading his Quran when he heard the knock on the door. Tony was not anticipating a visit from anybody. He hesitated before opening the door. Mr. Lawson felt a little sad after stepping inside the 10X10 room with a single bed and a small dresser. However, he had good news for Tony this time. Deon had wired five thousand dollars to Mr. Lawson and a one-way ticket to Miami for Tony to head down the next day. He couldn't believe that his luck had changed so fast. Tony hadn't seen five thousand dollars in cash his whole life. He just knew that something great was about to happen to him. Mr. Lawson was also given specific instructions to take Tony to Neiman Marcus to get fitted for a suit. Since they were running short on time, Mr. Lawson suggested that Tony get dressed and they drove to the Braintree mall to buy him a nice suit at Milton's. Mr. Lawson was practical. He didn't see any reason to spend so much money on a suit at Neiman Marcus when Tony could get a nice Italian-cut wool suit from Milton's. A complete outfit was purchased for Tony, including shoes, shirt, tie, socks and undergarments. Mr. Lawson brought him back to the shop to shave his bald pate. He was ready for his trip down to Miami.

Welcome To Miami

The sun was beaming when Deon showed up at the airport in the Range Rover to pick up Tony. A big smile flashed across Tony's face when he noticed the well-dressed Deon standing in the baggage area looking like a million bucks in a dark Italian tailored suit. Tony carried a handbag that contained his personal items. That was all he needed to carry because Deon had planned on taking him to the mall to shop, and to his personal tailor as well to get a few suits made for him. "How was the trip down?" Deon asked as the two men gave each other a brotherly hug. "Everything was fine. You're looking mighty dapper there, young man," Tony said proudly. "You don't look too bad yourself," Deon responded. There was a lot of catching up to do as the two men had not seen each other since Deon was released from prison. "How's everybody up top doing?" Deon asked. "You know how it is in there, everybody's trying to survive and hoping to be free like us one day," Tony said sadly. Deon had always affectionately called Tony just T. "T, I've been making some major moves since I came out, so you don't have to worry about a thing. I plan on looking out for you and help you get back on your feet. I can always use your wisdom, because you were like a father to me in there," he told him, referring to prison. "You don't owe me a thing. I did what I was supposed to do for my godchild. I know you don't know this, but your dad had told me he wanted me to be your godfather after you were born," Tony revealed. "Well, he couldn't pick a better man, and I appreciate you looking out for me," Deon told him graciously. "I'm proud of you, D," Tony said with pride. "I'm not looking for any handouts. I plan on working for mine. Whatever job you have available, I will do it earnestly and honestly," Tony told him. Deon smiled at the now wise Tony. "I'm sure there's a position for you in my organization, but I have to catch you up with what I've been doing," Deon said as he focused on the road.

The two drove straight to the mall for Tony to pick up some gear and other personal hygiene items he would need at the house. Their second stop was Deon's personal tailor. A dozen custom-designed suits in various conservative colors were ordered for Tony, as well as dress-shirts, handkerchiefs and ties to match the suits. While Deon wanted to help provide for Tony, Tony kept reinforcing that he didn't want any handouts. He wanted to repay Deon for everything that he was spending on him. Since Tony had become somewhat of a father figure for Deon when he was in prison, he was very in tune with Deon's mood. While talking about his business ventures on the way home with Tony, Deon was apprehensive about letting him know the situation with the mob. Right away Tony could sense that Deon was holding something back. "I know you ain't gonna hold out on your pops, you still consider me like pop, right?" Tony asked. "Man, you ain't never changed. I could never hide anything from you," Deon said while smirking. "Spill it. I know I just got out, but it doesn't mean that I won't get my hands dirty if I have to. You have to get dirty sometimes to stay on top, and I plan on keeping you on top. You're the only son I'll ever know, so you best get used to the idea that I'm not going to stop acting like a father to you," Tony said devotedly.

Deon understood that Tony had only been home less than a month and he didn't want to get him involved in something that would send him back to prison. "You know that I have no parole officer because I did all of my time. I don't have to watch over my back because of some parole fool I have to report to," Tony assured him. "It's not that. You should at least enjoy yourself for a few days before we get into all this business stuff. That's going to be around forever," Deon told him. "It's your call, but don't hesitate to talk to me whenever you're ready," Tony told him. He had been in prison for so long, he probably forgot what pussy felt like. The first order of the day was to get him a beautiful vixen or two to entertain him for the weekend, Deon thought.

Upon arrival at Deon's estate, Tony's mouth almost dropped to the floor. He couldn't believe his eyes. Deon had exceeded his expectations. The house, the cars, and working staff were something that Tony had seen only on television shows like Dynasty. He was intrigued and wanted to know how Deon was doing it all. After leading him to his personal suite on one wing of the house, Tony had to ask jokingly, "How many people did you kill to get a house like that?" "If I tell you, I'd have to kill you as well," Deon told him jokingly. "Make yourself comfortable. The crew is going to meet us in South Beach for dinner. If you need to freshen up, go ahead, but be ready for dinner by 8:00 PM. You might wanna wear one of your best suits from the bunch," Deon instructed before he left.

Meanwhile, Deon placed a call to Cindy to make sure that the "Welcome Home" party being planned for Tony at the luxurious Ritz Carlton was all set. Deon had put Cindy in charge of planning the party to ensure everything went accordingly. The ballroom at the Ritz Carlton was well decorated and a "Welcome Home Mr. Abdul Mustafa Muhammad" sign hung on the wall adjacent to the entrance of the ballroom. Party favors, balloons and the scantily clad women gave the party a Moulin Rouge cabaret theme. One of the hottest rap groups from the '80's, Whodini, also Tony's favorite group, was set to perform, along with Adina Howard and New York's hottest DJ, Funk Master Flex, was flown in to host the event. A lot of who's who in town was invited to the party. Trick Daddy, Too Live Crew Members, Flo Rida, Trina, members of the Cash Money crew and other celebrities arrived early for the red carpet event. Deon made many friends during the last year while his business flourished. Many of them came to show support for a man Deon referred to as his father and mentor.

Deon wore a black two-piece custom tailored, light wool suit, a crisp white cotton shirt, white handkerchief, and since cost was no object, John Lobb of London was the way to go with the shoes. From fitting to construction to the finest leathers and the highest shine, the process of making Deon's shoes took around seven months for the first pair, but they were worth the wait. Company reps make regular trips to the U.S. for fittings and Deon took advantage by ordering ten pairs of his favorite shoes in different colors and styles. That night, he went with a black pair of moccasins and wore no tie. Tony hadn't yet addressed the fact that he would like to be called Abdul with Deon yet, so Deon continued to refer to him as T. Tony wore a Canali Collection exclusive, Italian-designed six-button double breasted suit, made from the finest pure Super 200's wool in soft blue tones and subtle Prince of Wales, chalk-stripe and twilled styles--often rendered Ton Sur Ton--with contrasting wavy backgrounds with a striped soft brown tie and a pale blue striped shirt that he purchased from Saks Fifth Avenue. To compliment the suit, he wore a brown pair of the anti-label of high-end footwear, Tanino Crisci's subtle and stylish handmade Italian shoes, and a belt that matched the precise color of his shoes. The brothers looked like a million bucks and they were ready to take on the town. Tony had no idea about the "Surprise party" when he arrived at the Ritz Carlton. The Red Carpet event was full of flashing lights from the photographers and partygoers alike. Even the mayor was due to make a brief appearance at the party, considering the amount of money that Deon had donated to his campaign.

Tony walked into the room to a welcoming chant of, "Welcome home Mr. Abdul Mustafa Muhammad." Moments later, the crowd started singing, "He's a jolly good fellow," but the lyrics were changed to "He's a jolly Hoodfella." Tony was speechless, he had no idea that Deon would go all out for him like that. At the urging of the crowd, Tony decided to make a brief speech before the party commenced. "Today, I'm the happiest man, not because I'm free, but because I reconnected with the man that I've long considered my only son. I'm happy and proud of all his accomplishments and I would like to make a toast in honor of Deon," Tony said as he raised his champagne glass to the crowd. Deon joined in with a glass of water that he was sipping on. The first order of business was to introduce Tony to the rest of the crew before the party set off. Deon and the crew went to a private room, and one by one each member was introduced to Tony. However, Crusher gave a long-lasting hug to Tony because he hadn't seen him since he was released from prison. Tony was happy to see that Deon kept a tight-knit family and that success didn't change him as a person, but he was definitely a leader. Tony was especially happy to see Serena again.

While Deon had a couple of beautiful women on ice waiting to please Tony for the weekend, Tony had other plans. The ravishing looking Serena was breathtaking to him and she had all of his attention. Tony had matured as a man and one-night-stands were not his thing. Though it seemed wrong for him to have been lusting after his former best friend's woman, he didn't care. Sticky Fingers, Deon's dad, had been dead for three decades, and in no way did Tony want to disrespect him, but the chemistry between him and Serena was undeniable. The two ended up dancing the night away and catching up on old times, while Deon kept watch on them most of the night. It was only natural that the father figure in Deon's life would end up dating his biological mother. However, Tony didn't want any conflict, and neither did Serena.

My Mom and Tony?

Out of respect for Deon and Serena, Tony decided to ask for Deon's permission before he established anything remotely romantic under Deon's roof with his mother. Deon suspected the harmless flirting between his mother and Tony, but he never expected them to go full throttle so quickly into a relationship. Serena and Tony walked back to the same private room to have a personal conversation with Deon. "Well, son, we're calling you here because we're grown and we don't wanna be sneaking around behind your back trying to build a relationship," Serena said. Tony wanted to interject, but he waited until Serena spoke her piece before he spoke. "Deon, as far as I'm concerned, you're my son. I don't mean any disrespect by trying to date your mother. I've known Serena since we were kids and there has always been chemistry between us..." before he could complete his thoughts, Deon jumped in and said, "I don't really care what y'all do. Just don't put me in the middle of it if the shit hit the fan. I'm going back to the party to have a good time. You all are grown folks, I'm sure neither of you want to disappoint me," he said while smirking at them as he walked out of the room. Actually, when Serena and Mean T were kids, she initially had a crush on Mean T, but Sticky Fingers was a lot more aggressive than Mean T, so he ended up with Serena. Mean T decided to back off because he and Sticky Fingers were best friends. Serena revealed this little secret to Tony while they were dancing. Tony also revealed that he found her attractive back then, but he was too shy to say anything to her. As in most cases, nobody can stop destiny.

Mean T had always been a dedicated and loyal friend to Sticky Fingers, and he would've never crossed that line with Serena. He became a surrogate father to Deon in the most extreme place. Nevertheless, he was still a father figure in Deon's life for twenty years in prison. Without his protection and guidance, there was a very good chance that Deon would have had a harder time in prison. Deep down, Deon was a little happy that his mom and Tony were hooking up. He figured they both needed each other because he damn sure didn't plan on being around forever for them.

A Little Play Time

The party went over without any incidents. The two sexy women designated for Tony ended up going home with Smitty. He was overdue for some fun and he couldn't pass up on releasing the sexual frustration he had been carrying around with him for so long. The taller of two women grabbed Smitty's attention right away. He didn't even care to know her name while the rest of the men drooled over her. He just wanted to let go and have a night of pleasure once and for all. The light-skinned sister stood about 5ft 10 carrying a little over one hundred and forty pounds sans fat. Her nice round C-cup breasts were firm and perky, but her booty was her best asset; perfect in every shape and form. Her long flowing weave didn't even look fake, because she was the type of beauty to have that kind of long flowing hair. Her full lips, big brown eyes and button nose only added to the total vixen package she was. Smitty was surprised she had not been in a lot of rap videos, though she aspired to do so. Her five-inch heels and form fitting dress with the spaghetti lines on the side revealing she was not wearing any underwear drew stares from all the men at the party.

The other petite chocolate thunder could also hold her own in any beauty contest. She was just shy of 5 ft 1 inch tall and weighed a notch above 115lbs. Her dark complexion and beautiful, bright smile could light up a room. In fact, it did. This woman had more men and women looking her way than a celebrity among common folks. Deon must have handpicked her himself. Her curves were dangerous and appetizing. Her strong African features were good enough to command top billing on a billboard for a blockbuster film. Her firm round booty, toned legs, ripped arms and washboard stomach accessorized the beautiful shape bestowed upon her by The Man Upstairs. Her strut was to die for and even a gay man would dream of being with her, at least once. Smitty looked like the ultimate pimp walking out with the two women on his arms. Little did they know, they had their work cut out for them.

The lean looking Smitty never cracked a smile as he ushered the two women to the waiting Range Rover. Instead of going to the mansion, he drove straight to the Marriott hotel where a suite had been booked for Tony. The two women were impressed and at the same time giddy, because they hadn't anticipated such a young and good-looking client. "Y'all ready to have some fun?" Smitty uttered for the first time. The ladies were almost shocked that he could talk. They both couldn't be any older than twenty-five, but they seemed professional enough to know what was going down. "What kind of fun do you like to have?" inquired Ms. Chocolate. 'The kind of fun that you'd never imagine," Smitty answered. The intrigue was killing the women and they couldn't wait to get to the hotel to put it on the young buck. They even started playing with themselves in the truck to entice young Smitty. The moaning and groaning back and forth between the two women while they fondled themselves had no effect on Smitty as he stayed focused on the road. However, like any man, his dick was hard as steel and the light skinned girl sitting in the front with him could see his protruding dick through his pants. She got a little nervous as she estimated Smitty was packing a good eleven inches or maybe more.

Ms. Caramel reached for Smitty's dick and decided to get a headstart. Smitty reclined the seat for comfort and allowed her to take his long, fat dick in her mouth while Ms. Chocolate looked on. "How does it taste?" Ms. Chocolate asked with curiosity. "Very appetizing," Ms. Caramel revealed between licks. Smitty never cracked a smile. He kept his focus on the road while enjoying Ms. Caramel's tongue twirling around his dick. They arrived at the Marriott in no time. Smitty held his jacket in front of him to keep his bulge obscure from the walking patrons in the lobby. The two women were snickering at his attempt to be inconspicuous.

By the time Smitty slid the card through the slot to open the door, the two women were already unbuckling his pants and ready to devour him once they got inside. He took off his tie and used it to tie the women's hands together while they faced each other. He ordered them to make out with each other while he sat on the bed to watch. After the ladies kissed, caressed and fondled each other for a while, Smitty decided to join in. Since he was slightly taller than Ms. Caramel, it was easier for him to start with her over by the dresser. She was bent over the dresser while Ms. Chocolate was underneath her sucking on her breasts. Smitty slipped on an extra large condom and slowly penetrated Ms. Caramel from behind. His strokes were nice and slow as he palmed Ms. Caramel's ass, savoring her pussy like a long lost treasure. Meanwhile, Ms. Chocolate continued to entertain herself by taking one of Ms. Caramel's nipples in her mouth as she moaned from Smitty's strokes. "Fuck me, daddy," she begged while Smitty smacked her ass hard enough to sting. Ms. Caramel's pink hole stretched beyond imagination as Smitty went deep-digging for the bottom of her well. "Your dick feels so good, daddy," she cooed. "I want some too," Ms. Chocolate announced upon hearing Ms. Caramel's words. Smitty was silent and focused as he caressed and pounced on Ms. Caramel's pussy. He stopped long enough to untie the two women so he could have them both bent over on the edge of the bed so he could fuck both of them.

He switched from Ms. Caramel to Ms. Chocolate. He slowly inserted his dick as her legs started trembling. Her pussy was a little tighter than expected, so Smitty took his time easing his entire dick inside her pussy. "Oh my God, I'm cumming!" she screamed at the very first stroke. Smitty must've hit her G-spot. She arched her ass up against his dick and started grinding at a fast speed. Meanwhile, Smitty had his middle and index finger inside Ms. Caramel while his thumb caressed her anus. The symphony of pleasure coming from the two women was music to Smitty's ears. He stood still to allow Ms. Chocolate the pleasure of climaxing on his dick and no sooner did Ms. Caramel start screaming that she was coming while massaging her own clit, with Smitty's fingers in her pussy and ass. After the two women came, Smitty sat on the edge of the bed, pulled his condom off and commanded both of them to suck his dick simultaneously. The image alone was enough to have him succumb to their prowess, and that he did minutes later. Ms. Caramel and Ms. Chocolate took turns alternating their tongues around the shaft of Smitty's dick until he could no longer stand it. They squeezed every ounce of semen out of his dick and rubbed it on their bodies like they were porn stars. Though the two women were paid for by Deon through an agency, Smitty decided to give them each a one hundred dollar tip. The two of them wrote their numbers down on a piece of paper and promised that he would never have to pay to see them again. Smitty had proven that he was more pleasure than business.

Business As Usual

It was time to get back to business the following day. Deon had decided to tell Abdul about the mob trying to muscle their way into his pockets. After hearing everything that went down, Abdul told Deon, "I'm gonna need some time to think of a way outta this, but you gotta be willing to die for your empire. This is an empire that you have built and you can't just let anybody come in and take it away from you." Deon stood there and listened, but he could also read Abdul's face. He knew Abdul was a logical thinker who thought things out first before acting. Deon had never faced an adversary so powerful in the past. The mob was nothing to mess with in South Beach and Deon knew that he had better be ready to put his life on the line if he didn't want to give in to the mob's demands. "We're gonna have to try to buy ourselves a little time, because the mob is a lot more organized than any other crime syndicate on the streets. Meanwhile, let's try to keep them occupied while we figure out what to do," Abdul revealed. "How we gonna do that?" Deon asked confusingly. "Well, we're gonna call another meeting with them to make our business dealings official. While on lockdown, I had the opportunity to befriend a couple of wise guys. They like to think they're businessmen, and we're gonna make them feel exactly as they wish," Abdul assured Deon. However, Deon was still a little confused because he didn't want to give the mob not even one red cent. "Son, sometimes you have to give a little so you can gain a whole lot more. We're gonna have to give the mob a little of what they want until we are in a position to annihilate them," Abdul told him. "Why should I have to give these assholes a cent of my money?" Deon questioned. "You're a better thinking man than this. Right now, you're acting on sheer emotion and bravado. I know you didn't build this empire thinking with your strength, you have to use your mind to win this battle before it becomes a war," Abdul calmly told him.

Deon had been the leader of his crew for so long, he never needed guidance from anybody to act or react to a situation. He always went with his instincts and gut, but this time, it would take more than that. "First, I need you to call a meeting with the crew to make them aware of the situation. We're not going to give them every detail of what's going on, but we have to make them aware of the mob and that we are now dealing with them," Abdul told him in a non-threatening way. Deon had lost his cool but for a minute. He knew he had to be reasonable and it was time for him to listen to Abdul. It was almost like a father passing his wisdom on to his son. Though the mob was going to be cutting into the profits of the Hoodfellas enterprise, it had to be done that way for the benefit of the long term prosperity of the business.

The doors opened everyday and it was business as usual. Deon also met with everybody in the crew and made them aware that they might have a visitor or two from the mob every week to collect their share of the business. Meanwhile, there were setbacks. The Hoodfellas had to change their spending habits as well as their exposure in South Beach. They couldn't allow people to know their strength or weakness. Smitty especially had a hard time with the new arrangements, because he felt he could walk into the mob's territory like Rambo and erase every single one of them single-handedly. His heroic efforts and brave heart would have to wait. Crusher was just as mad because the Hoodfellas had never been pushed around before. They were fighters and soldiers and did not fear the enemy or death. Cooler heads had to prevail and the strategy for battle had to change. While it's never okay to allow somebody to rob you of what you feel is rightfully yours, Deon also knew that was part of the game. Abdul had to help him realize that. Serena wasn't too happy about the move, but she understood where Abdul was coming from and decided to go with it.

Meanwhile, the plan to deal the mob was being put together thoroughly behind closed doors, only Deon and Abdul were involved in the brainstorming. Abdul wanted to make sure Deon kept his position with the crew as leader. He only wanted to assist and he never wanted to impose his will or knowledge in front of the crew. He understood that Deon couldn't be undermined even in the most compromising position. The crew had to follow their leader's directives and Abdul wanted to make sure that happened. The situation got so exciting and tense that Abdul reverted back to Mean T, the criminal. All his Muslim teachings in jail were out the window as he embarked on this new journey in crime. Smitty was growing impatient with the mob and kept wondering why the Hoodfellas hadn't switched to attack mode yet to teach the mob a lesson. It was time for a one on one talk with Smitty. "Smitty, I understand your frustration and believe me, I'm not happy about giving our money to some damn greasy hair Guito, but we can't take the same approach with this situation that we always took. I'm trying my best to teach you how to be a soldier as well as a businessman, because you need to learn both to survive out here. This is new territory for us and we can't give these goons the opportunity to take over our enterprise," Deon sternly told Smitty. "They got guns, we got guns. They can pull a trigger, we can pull a trigger. What makes them so powerful then?" Smitty asked ignorantly. "It's a lot more than guns. These people are connected in high places and they can set us up. They have judges, cops, lawyers, politicians and everything else on their payroll. We have to deal with them a different way. When we attack them, they can't know it came from us, understand?" Smitty reluctantly shook his head. "I just need you to be a little patient. You will get a chance to shoot your gun, shooter," Deon said while laughing and rubbing the top of Smitty's head. They dapped each other before walking away.

Casey

While trouble was brewing in Florida, the Chinese Connection was trying to find the men who shot No Neck and Short Dawg. Those men were brave enough to think that they could get away with killing two of Deon's closest pals. They had gotten word that Deon and the Hoodfellas fled Boston, and they thought they had something to do with that. They figured the killing of No Neck and Short Dawg instilled enough fear in the Hoodfellas that they decided to get out of dodge. They were wrong. Deon had paid his Chinese associates handsomely to deliver the heads of those killers on a stick and the Chinese Connection always delivered.

Casey, the dude that Short Dawg grew up with who ended up crossing him, earned the nickname Case because he was always in court and beat his cases every time. Case was living the high life in Boston. He had gone into hiding immediately after killing Short Dawg and No Neck, but after he got word that the Hoodfellas left town, his head started to swell up. He used that incident to gain control of the streets of Boston. He was involved in every hustle and illegal activity on the street. In his own head, he had become untouchable. Case wasn't all that creative in his business approach. Though Deon didn't leave behind a blueprint for his success, Case took it upon himself to try to emulate Deon in every way possible, with the addition of taking on the street corner hustlers and forcing them to give him a piece of their pie.

Case never left his house without the twin .45 Lugar he carried around his waist. He instilled fear and ruled with an iron fist. His right hand man was Big Nate, a dude he's known since he was three years old and former Golden Glove champion; he was a knockout specialist. His dream of becoming a heavyweight boxer was deflated when another up-and-coming boxer gave him a glass jaw. His other friend, Fat Pat, was also a childhood friend with a thirst for blood. Fat Pat was intimidating in size, but he couldn't fight to save his life, due to his asthma. However, he was trigger happy. They all grew up in Orchard Park Housing Projects and came up with a taste of the good life in their mouths. Short Dawg presented them with the biggest opportunity they ever had, but greed forced them to stab Short Dawg in the back. Now they felt the streets were theirs and they drove around in a darkly-tinted, S-class Mercedes Benz, collecting money daily from their victims. Life was good for Case and his two flunkies, their reputation preceded them. They ruled by brute force and they left their marks on every victim.

After the incident with the Hoodfellas, Case was facing multiple murder and conspiracy charges, but he beat the case in court because no witnesses showed up in court to testify against him. He had put the word out in the hood that if anybody came forward to testify, their whole family would be found in Houghton's pond with bullet holes all over their bodies. Apparently, people took his threats seriously. He started to believe he was a Teflon Don and started wreaking havoc on the streets. He also became a Kingpin and every small time drug dealer from New Bedford to Boston had to get their supply from him. The one guy who thought he was tough enough to stand against Case learned the hard way that Case was a basket case. The guy was an up-and-coming Cape Verdean dealer from New Bedford who had made a name for himself on the streets of his neighborhood. When Case approached him about buying from him, he pulled out his pistol and chased Case out of town, unloading his gun on the bulletproof Mercedes. Case ran out of town, but came back with a gang of killers. The young drug dealer's body was mutilated and he was left hanging on a rope behind a building with his eyeballs missing. That action solidified Case's position in New Bedford as he aimed to take over the city's drug trade.

Case soon moved north towards Brockton where he did random "drive-bys," killing young slingers on the street for no reason, before approaching them with his proposal. He would later threaten to kill, or killed the suppliers before taking their spots altogether. Case was on a roll, muscling his way through the drug trade like Pablo Escobar. He started in the southern part of Massachusetts first, because he knew the guys out there were a little softer than the dealers in Boston. Word traveled quickly and by the time Case reached Boston, they were ready for him.

Orchard Park has always been one of the roughest projects in Boston, but Case didn't have a stronghold on it. As a matter of fact, most of the people in Orchard Park Housing Projects thought Case was soft as a kid. He used to get his ass whipped regularly and he would always run from a fight. It wasn't until after he did a bid at the DYS, a youth facility in Boston, that he grew enough balls to stand up to his peers in the projects. While at DYS, his back was against the wall and he no choice but to fight, and fight he did. Case started getting nice with his hands and by the time his bid was over, he had earned the respect of some of the toughest guys in the jail. However, when he came home no one cared about his reputation in the joint. There were guys who tested him and some of them even bested him. He wasn't that good yet. Case knew he had to be even better at Orchard Park than he was at DYS. He continued to hone his fighting skills, but more importantly, he became a ruthless assassin who didn't mind killing anybody who tested, or went against him. He would later form a crew of killers for hire. Case and his boys were knocking off husbands, wives, lovers, enemies and foes for anybody who paid the right price. In the hood, the right price was no more than $10,000.00. It was good business considering the amount of hate that was going around in Boston. Case vacated his plans to take over the streets of Boston temporarily.

Case's big payday would come when Short Dawg approached him with a million dollar proposition to help out the Hoodfellas. He jumped at the opportunity, but his greedy, evil eyes figured he could score even bigger to put him at the top, if he crossed his trusted friend, Short Dawg. Unfortunately for Case, Short Dawg was a man of his word and only the million dollar payment owed to him was in the van on the day of delivery. He killed Short Dawg and No Neck for no reason. They had never planned to cross him. It was a business deal and everybody was supposed to go their separate ways. However, Case decided to leave a mark on his head by killing Short Dawg, and No Neck.

Case decided to go back to his greedy, and power hungry ways, but he was doing it in Boston this time. Since the incidents in New Bedford, Brockton and the murder of Short Dawg and No Neck, Case's status went from hardcore gangster, to cold-blooded murderer. However, not everyone was afraid of him. The Young G's crew had been controlling most of Mission Hill Projects drug trade for the last three years. Every member of the crew was eating well, and they stood strong against any foe who tried to penetrate their turf. They weren't just Young G's, they were also young gunners who blazed murdering trails all over Boston to solidify their stance in the projects.

When Case and his crew tested one of the Young G's in Mission Hill, he was met with a hail of bullets by a crew he didn't see coming. He thought his intimidating force of two packed Chevy Suburbans with twelve armed men was enough to descend upon the Young G's and run them out of their territory. The lone young gangster standing on the corner didn't even blink an eye when Case pulled up and rolled down his window to tell him, "Look, there's a new sheriff in town, you gonna have to get down with us or get got." It only took one hand signal for the other Young

G's to strap up and start unloading their weapons at the two trucks that were parked along the side street. Scared gangsters from the trucks scrambled as bullets flew from rooftops, bushes and behind parked cars. At the end of the mayhem, the Young G's had killed five of Case's men, and even Case himself was hit in the leg as tires peeled and rubber burned when they scurried to safety.

However, the Young G's victory would be short-lived as Case regrouped and came back with an army a few weeks later to wipe out the Young G's. He became a strategist after he came out of the hospital. As his life flashed before his eyes, Case knew his intimidating factor didn't instill fear in everybody. He had to devise new tactics to go to war with the Young G's. Plenty of young women were hired to work as spies against the Young G's to reveal their hiding gunners and their hideouts. These young women were like street whores as they lay down with the enemy for a handsome amount of money paid by Case. One by one, the Young G's saw their destiny at the barrel of a 9MM Glock with a silencer from their hiding locations. The element of surprise worked perfectly on the night Case and his crew decided to annihilate them once and for all. The tough leader of the Young G's was dragged in the middle of the streets and stripped butt naked before his arms and legs were chopped off and left to bleed to death. The equalizer for snitches would be the same fate the Young G's leader suffered at the hand of Case.

After taking out the Young G's, Case not only hardened his presence in the hood, he was the god who ruled with a deathly fist. Everyone feared him and he felt he could go anywhere and be respected. His army of armed men ensured his security, and whenever Case had any suspicion that anybody in his crew was a snitch, he shot them point blank. Everyone had to prove their loyalty to him, except for his two main men, who had been hustling with him from the start. The three of them had garnered enough bodies that they were all certified killers. They trusted each other with their lives.

The Chinese Connection

There was a lot of money on the table for the Chinese Connection. Deon had promised them an additional two million dollars after they completed the job. All conventional methods were thrown out the door as the Chinese Connection set out to find Case and his crew. In a situation so deadly, Tommy Li would be wise to use his male enforcers to do the job, but this time he had to go with his instincts and put his trust in the fierce women in his crew. The trio of women was perfect for the job. Mae Ling, Lisa Ming and Dina Wong were the best weapon in Tommy's arsenal. They always worked together and knew each other's instincts and thoughts at all times. They trained with the best martial artist back in China and also had weapon training by one of the US Army's best marksmen. They knew how to use everything from a handgun to a grenade launcher.

Case didn't make it too difficult for people to find him. His cockiness and ego for power made him available to every weakling that wanted to kill him, but the problem was that he instilled fear in people and believed that the fear protected him from harm. As usual, Case and his two cohorts hung out at Club Venue in Boston, near Chinatown. The three women had been watching his every move for the past three months. They had his schedule down to a science. Though Deon was the financier of the hit on Case and his boys, the three women soon realized they could manage a score of their own, independent of the Chinese Connection while following Case. As much as Case tried to switch up his routine on a weekly basis, the end result was always the same. He picked up the most money from the different drug houses in Boston on Mondays, as well as drug supplies from his Colombian supplier on Monday evenings.

Everything seemed normal when the three ladies moved toward the bar to order drinks for themselves. They looked like sisters, as the three of them wore tight-fitting dresses in black, white and red that left very little to the imagination. Panties were not an option that evening when the ladies got dressed. Panty lines, whether thong or boy-shorts, would take away from the dresses. The five-inch heels these women sported made them look like supermodels fresh off a runway. Mae Ling wore the hot red dress because she had the hottest body of the three. Lisa wore black to accentuate what few curves she had, and Dina wore white to keep intact her innocence. However, all three of them were cold blooded killers. Only a blind man would miss these three ladies when they strutted to the bar. Case noticed them right away from the comfort of his cushioned seat in the VIP section. As a regular baller who spent thousands of dollars at the club every week, he was known by the club owner and security, as well as the bartenders. He signaled for the bartender to put the ladies' drinks on his tab and in addition, offered to buy a bottle of Dom Perignon while he invited them to join him in the VIP area.

So far so good, the ladies thought, as Case fell for the bait. The chickenheads around Case were wearing screw faces as the three beautiful young women made their way to the VIP to join Case and his men. Though the chickenheads who had already joined Case prior to these women had bodies and faces that could land them video gigs, Case was intrigued by the exotic looks of the Asian women. "I ain't never had no Asian pussy," he whispered to his boy, Nate, on his right, as the ladies approached. Fat Pat was all smiles because he knew that there was no way Case was going to be fucking all of the women by himself. He was down for whatever crummy leftover that was sent his way.

The usual order of business for Case and his boys at the club every Sunday was to get new pussy. They would spend any amount of money as long as it netted them pussy. Most of these women didn't care. They just wanted to be with a baller; looks or profession played no role in their decision. However, this time getting the pussy wouldn't be so easy. The jealous chickenheads were escorted out of VIP without any warning as Case tried to concentrate on the Asian persuasions before him. "How ya doin', Ma?" he said, letting them know from the jump he was a street dude. Mae Ling was his first choice and she jumped in to let him know that she enjoyed his street vernacular, "Wow, I like the way you talk. You sound all Hip Hop and shit." Case smiled from ear to ear while he tried to get his Jay Z swag on. "So you like Hip Hop, huh?" he asked. "We love Hip Hop. That's why we're here," Mae Ling assured him. It was almost as if the ladies had been practicing their moves in a dance studio somewhere in somebody's basement for a while. Lisa was all up on Nate, while Dina was shaking her ass against Fat Pat's gut. The guys weren't really dancers, so they just leaned back while they enjoyed the back view of the ladies in their tight dresses. Though the women had very little ass, they appeared sexy because the dresses were so fitting. The onlookers in the predominantly Black club couldn't help taking glances at the ladies as they danced seductively with Case and his boys. They stood out like sore thumbs in a club crowded with black women.

The champagne was flowing all night long as Case made plans to take the ladies out to get food at a spot near the club afterwards. Their minds were on pussy while the women had their minds on killing them, but not before robbing them of their money. After breakfast, the ladies followed Case in their own car, as he took them to his spot in Quincy. This was his private domain where he never dared to bring the chickenheads he met at the club. He wanted to impress the Asian women, so he took them to his most luxurious spot. He thought his game was flawless as he pointed out his Range Rover in the parking garage as he parked his Benz next to it. The condo was not purchased in Case's name, but he laced it out like he was Frank Lucas. The marble floors invaded the foyer all the way back to the kitchen where the granite countertop was customized to match the floor. The stainless steel appliances were the latest designs and top notch brand that was available on the market. The four-bedroom, five-bath pad was outfitted with the latest Italian furnishings. The living room, dining room and every bedroom had the shiny Italian lacquer finished furniture. The ladies acted like they were impressed, but they had pegged these guys to be typical drug dealers and their taste in clothes and furniture made the case for them. Case took them around to show them every room in the pad, except for one room in the back. The six of them chatted until the wee hours in the morning, but none of the ladies gave up the ass. Case got the furthest with Mae Ling when she spread her legs so he could see her pinkness. "If you play your cards right, maybe you can get some of this tomorrow," Mae Ling whispered in his ear. Impressed with his own impression on the ladies, Case made plans to see Mae Ling, the following day, which was Monday.

If there was one vice that Case possessed besides a huge appetite for money, it was his even bigger appetite for pussy. He was consumed by two things in life: money and pussy, but pussy had more of an affect on him than money. He could always get money, but conquering pussy was his thing. He had to conquer this Asian chick to satisfy his own ego. He wanted her so bad; he left very little time between his money pick-up and the time he had to meet with her for dinner the next day.

Confident that his lies as a businessman in import and export won the ladies over, Case knew he had to step his game up to get some Chinese pussy the next time he saw Mae Ling. However, Mae Ling warned him that she wouldn't go on a date with him alone. She wanted her girlfriends to come along. The ladies lied to Case and his friends and told them they were students at MIT. The ladies pulled off the college student story without a hitch. Case and his men believed they were about to turn out some MIT students the following day.

The Heat is On

The hot weather in Miami wasn't letting up, but even more, the mob was bringing the heat hotter than ever. To reinforce their demands, they dropped the mutilated body of one of Deon's employees in front of his office at seven o'clock in the morning. He was a young man named Mike, around twenty two years, old who detailed the luxury vehicles for the business. He was not part of the squabble going on between The Hoodfellas and the mob, but he fell victim to it. He was shot in the back of the head before they mutilated his body. This was a costly example and Deon knew that he had to act quickly. The soldiers were ready for an all-out war, but they were outgunned. Deon had to keep a cooler head even in the face of tragedy. He couldn't afford to lose another person from his family. Mike never signed up for his fate, but that's what he was served. He was only there to do a job, and he did it well. There was no reason for him to be murdered.

An investigation ensued because a dead body was found on the premises of the Luxurious Life, LLC. Deon's cooperation was necessary in order to avoid going to jail for a murder he didn't commit. The cops wanted to find a motive for Mike's death, but none was immediately found. Mike had been an exemplary employee, and Deon even gave him a raise a week before he was killed. The cops promised to continue their investigation, but Deon or anybody on his staff was not on the suspect list yet.

The Capo showed up at Deon's office two days later with guns blazing in his hand with four of his soldiers and two associates. "I guess you must've thought we were playing with you Moolies when we approached you with our business proposal," Giuseppe Russo, the hungry Capo who wanted to show his boss he was worth the promotion to Capo. Crusher, Smitty, Deon and Mean T looked on as the man spoke. The look in their eyes was so sharp it could cut across glass. Unfazed by the intimidating looks of the Hoodfellas, the Capo announced, "You's now in for a twenty percent stake every month and I'll be back tomorrow for the first payment," as he backed out of the office and loaded into two waiting Cadillac Devilles.

The Hoodfellas assumed Mike's dead body was the mob's way of reinforcing their demands. However, Giuseppe made no mention of the dead body because the coroner had already picked up the body and the crime scene was no longer there when they arrived to the office. "Man, I know we ain't gonna let these Guito bastards get away with killing Mike, right?" Smitty said angrily. Smitty and Mike were close in age and they had developed a relatively close friendship since Mike was hired. Deon's glazed eyes looked over to Mean T and then over to Smitty before he made his angry announcement, "We're gonna kill every single one of these bastards even if my life depends on it. No one is gonna come into our house and disrespect us and get away with it!" "That's what I'm talking about" Smitty and Crusher echoed. Mean T said nothing as he continued to observe the body language of Deon's crew and taking inventory of them. "Can I speak to you privately, Deon?" Mean T asked. Deon asked his crew to leave him alone in the office with Mean T. "I see you have some real emotional soldiers that are down with you, but you can't take them into a killing field against the mob. These men will eat your crew for breakfast and get away with it. I know what they've done to your worker is wrong, but we gotta fight to win. This is going to be more of a psychological battle than physical. We're gonna have to leave our emotions at the door if we want to win this war. You have got to find a way to calm your troops down, so we can teach these Guinea bastards not to ever fuck with a black business again." Deon stood there and listened intently while he allowed his anger to subside.

"What are we gonna do then, T? I have a group of angry soldiers out there who want to go to war, not just because of Mike, but because of their own safety. We don't know when these bastards are gonna strike again. We can't let our guards down and allow them another score against us. What Am I supposed to do?" Deon asked, clueless. Mean T knew that at the time Deon needed a few words of encouragement that he could be victorious against the mob, but he also cautioned, "In every war, there's always casualties on both sides." The Hoodfellas would have to make sure they were on the shorter end of the casualties. "You already know that I'm a warrior and I never back down from a good fight, but serving thirty years in prison has also taught me to use my mind to win a few of my battles. We cannot react hastily to their action. Trickery and the element of surprise is what we need in order to win this war," Mean T warned. The new plan to deal with the mob had to be expedited and Deon had to make sure he kept his soldiers calm before the storm.

Lights, Camera, Action!

The tight dresses that the ladies donned the night before were no more. This time, they wore dresses that barely covered their asses and tits and carried purses that were a little bigger than normal. Mae Ling and her girls stood right in front of the surveillance camera, allowing Case and his boys to take inventory of their skimpy outfits, shielding the background from view after ringing Case's doorbell. The strategically placed surveillance cameras were at the front and back door of the building. The men enjoyed the clear access view of the ladies on their big screen television. The surveillance system was hooked up to the TV and automatically activated when the doorbell rang. The girls took notice of this the night before, because Fat Pat had to run back to the car to retrieve something, and Case was showing off the surveillance system to them. The plan to meet at Case's place instead of the restaurant was perfect. Mae Ling made it seem like she needed to work up an appetite before going out to eat with Case and he fell right into her trap. "Sure, we can meet at my spot for drinks, smoke some weed before we head out," he concurred. "That sounds good, I hope you have some good chronic because me and my girls get real loose after smoking a good joint," Mae Ling told him. Case had his boys go around Boston the whole day looking for the most potent chronic they could find. He just knew he was gonna get some pussy and even possibly an orgy with the Asian chicks. He played right into her hand as she told him, "I love big dicks, but the Asian men I've been with have little dicks, I love sucking and I love fucking all night long," she confided to him. "That sounds good. We're gonna have some fun tonight," he said with a Kool Aid smile through the phone. "I hope your boys have big dicks because my friends love to fuck too. We've never been with black guys before, but my white friends tell me you guys are good with your big dicks," Mae Ling told Case, to fuck with his head. 'Well you know, once you go black you never go back. I know I have a nice, big, sweet dick for you, but I don't know about my boys. If I have to, I guess I'll be pleasing all three of you," he said jokingly. "Oh that sounds good. A foursome, that'll be fun," Mae Ling played along. "I guess I will see you ladies at eight o'clock tonight. I have to take care of some business right now," he said before hanging up the phone.

Not only was Case about to collect almost a million dollars from the streets that day, he had his mind set on some new pussy he'd never tasted before. He hustled hard for the finer things in life and nothing was worth more than fine, new pussy. His boys were right next to him as he talked to Mae Ling, so they all knew the expectation for the night. However, Nate did question whether or not the girls were cops. Case and his boys' business dealings had only been with black people, and black women for sex, for the most part. They had no angle on these high-class Asian chicks. The last time something like this happened, they were at a club in Providence, Rhode Island, where they met a group of white girls that they ended up taking back to the hotel with them. The white girls were easy, so they were all hoping for the same outcome with the Asian chicks, but Nate was a little leery of the ladies. "Man, we didn't even check these chicks to see if they're cops," Nate said worriedly to Case. "Man, these chicks ain't no damn cops the way they were shaking their ass. What cop you know gonna let you take a look at her pussy?" Case asked Nate. Fat Pat immediately moved in to dap Case for the comment and said, "Yo, the way Shawty was grinding that ass on me, ain't no way she a cop." "Yo, Shawty showed you her pussy for real?" Nate curiously asked. "Hell yeah! That shit was nice and pink with all the baby black hair nicely trimmed. I'm fucking me some Chinese pussy tonight!" Case announced.   Nate's mind was at ease once Case revealed that Mae Ling had exposed herself to him.

Case's first meeting was in Bridgewater where he met a Cape Verdean dude who left Nate a black backpack filled with money in the bathroom stall of a McDonald's restaurant. Nate left behind a similar backpack for the guy. The money collection went on all day from Bridgewater to Boston, like a Creflo Dollar church service. By the time the guys were done collecting, they had enough money to leave the street alone for a while, but that wasn't in the plans.

Eight o'clock couldn't arrive soon enough. Case and his boys jumped eagerly to their feet when they heard the doorbell ring at eight o'clock on the dot. The girls had arrived and they dressed like they were ready for action, but not the kind the guys were looking forward to. The minute the girls set foot inside the condo, Nate said, "Damn, where ya'll going with these big ass bags? We ain't going shopping or nothing," he cracked as the ladies headed straight to the bathroom. All three of the guys were in the living room with blunts rolled, drinks on ice and hard dicks ready to penetrate these chicks. Unfortunately, what transpired in the next five minutes could've only been prevented if these men didn't let their guards down because of fine pussy. All three women stepped out of the bathroom with guns drawn and silencers attached to each weapon. "Take your motherfucking clothes off!" Mae Ling ordered them to do. Case couldn't believe his eyes. "I ain't trying to get stuck by no Chinese bitches!" Fat Pat exclaimed while reaching for his 9mm handgun. No sooner did he reach, a bullet pierced right through the middle of his head and split his dome open. His limp body dropped to the floor as Nate said, "I told you not to trust these bitches." Mae Ling was the only shooter when Fat Pat got hit, but Lisa didn't find Nate's statement too entertaining, so she busted two caps in his knees. He started screaming in pain like a little bitch. "Shut the fuck up!" Dina ordered. "Now show us the money and we'll be on our way," Mae Ling told Case. "Oh shit, these bitches are here to rob us, Chinese motherfucking stick-up bitches?" Nate questioned. Another bullet pierced through the back of his head as Lisa said, "I told you to shut the fuck up." Case was the last man standing and he knew that he had better do what the ladies said. "Where are you hiding the money?" Mae Ling asked. "What money? I ain't got no money here," Case lied. The ladies already knew that the money was brought in because they had been tagging Case and his boys since earlier in the day. "I'm only gonna ask you once more. If you don't show me where you're hiding the money, you're gonna die a slow death," Mae Ling warned.

The serious look on Mae Ling's face was scary enough for Case to wet himself. "Whoever sent you, I can pay you double what they're paying you," Case offered. I'm gonna count to five, if you don't tell me where the money is, the first bullet is going straight to your right eye," Mae Ling said calmly. "Ok, the money is in the back room," Case said as he pointed to the room. All three ladies unloaded their weapons in unison after Case revealed where the money was. After killing him, the girls opened the door to let two Chinese guys into the apartment. They dragged the three bodies into the bathroom and severed all three heads and placed them in a plastic bag while the ladies stayed put in the living room. "We're all done," said one of the guys when he emerged from the bathroom holding a plastic, seemingly with a head or two in it, while the other guy carried another. "We're gonna stay here to clean up. We'll meet you back in town," Mae Ling told them.

Mae Ling and the girls went to the back room and collected every single dollar bill of Case's money. In all, they walked away with almost ten million dollars, which they split amongst themselves. This job was more than worth it, as they reported to their boss they only found two million dollars in the house, of course less the ten they split amongst them. It was expected of them to report the money to the organization that they worked for, but who said there had to be honor among thieves.

Cornered

Deon was no sucker! There was no way he was going to start making good on the mob's demands anymore. Retaliation was in order and he had better find a way to help convince the mob he was ready to go toe to toe with them. Feeling like their backs were against the wall, Tony and Deon devised a plan to take out a couple of the mob's associates as a concession for Mike's death. To concede was to retaliate twice as hard and that's exactly what Deon and the Hoodfellas did. A couple of the mob associates were well-known in South Beach, and they didn't hide their love for Hip Hop, especially the younger members. Sobe Live was the hottest spot in South Beach and the women came in droves. Three of the wannabe "made men" who were with Giuseppe when he showed up at Deon's office practically lived at the club on Monday night's college night party. The young impressionable college girls put out easily and these three mafia thugs always scored. Through his own street connections in Miami, Deon was able to find out their hangout and a fifty-thousand-dollar bounty was put on their head. The meanest street gang in South Florida was the Dog Pound Posse and Deon became an associate of theirs the day after the mob left his office. The word was quickly spread on the street about the bounty. It took less than forty eight hours for the gang to collect the bounty money.

The three Italian wanna-be mobsters never made it home after leaving the club with three white young ladies. The women weren't harmed, but the three guys were mutilated so badly that they were unrecognizable to family members. The mob was pissed and somebody had to pay. Giuseppe never questioned the fact that Deon had everything to do with the mutilation of his men. The gruesome pictures of the act were found in the Miami Herald. Ears had been chopped off one of the victims; another victim had his eyes pulled out of the socket and one of the third victim's testicles was cut off in a visibly painful manner. "I want the fucking moolie's head responsible for this on a stick!" Giuseppe announced to his flunky soldiers. The mob was out for blood and they didn't wait long to paint the town red.

Usually Smitty went out with the girls to open the office early, but he chose to stay in bed this particular day. "Papi, you ready to go open the office with us?" Maribel said through the door after knocking. Since Smitty didn't open the door, she turned the knob to find a knocked-out Smitty still in bed. It was unusual because Smitty was always the first one up. However, he suggested for her to get Evelyne or Rosie to help open the office. Maribel followed Smitty's suggestion, and got Rosie up to help her. The two ladies made their way out to the office in a new Chrysler M that Deon had purchased for them. As Maribel opened the front door of the office, all she heard was the screeching tires of a Lincoln Towncar as it came to a halt while three dark-haired and olive-skinned dudes came out with automatic weapons and started unloading on her. Rosie was still in the car trying to make her way out, but she didn't stand a chance either. She shot one of the men in the arm, but that was all she could do as bullets hit the front glass and side of the car from both ends. The two women died instantly and the news copters descended upon them within minutes of the shooting. It was mayhem in South Beach as every news station in Miami was scrambling for a witness to get a lead on the story.

Deon was still at home when two of his faithful team members were murdered in the dawn of morning. Deon had a habit of watching the news every morning before he left the house. "We have breaking news from Channel 4. Two women have been found shot dead in front of the office of the Luxurious Life, LLC. This is the second time in two weeks that police have discovered dead bodies in front of this thriving company. No information has been released about the victims as police continue to investigate the murder scene," the anchor woman reported. Deon quickly jumped out of bed and placed a phone call to his high-priced Jewish lawyer. "Epstein, I'm sure you've heard it on the news by now. Meet me at my office in forty five minutes…and prepare a statement for the cops and the public as well,'" Deon told him before hanging up the phone.

The Setup

Deon's lawyers had to act as publicists to divert the attention away from the successful business that the Hoodfellas worked so hard to establish. "We want to help assist the police catch the culprit who committed this heinous crime in any possible way that we can. Any information from the public will be appreciated. Meanwhile, we are going to set up a fund in the names of the victims and a scholarship program to help curb this violent behavior going on in Miami. Our children need more education and less guns. That is the belief of the president of The Luxurious Life, LLC, Mr. Deon Cambpell, who's a strong advocate for education," the lawyers released to the press. Deon didn't want his business to be associated with any kind of crime enterprise. He wanted to appear as legit as possible to the police and the public. Of course, there were many questions to be answered and his corporation was now being investigated by the police. Fortunately, Tweak's mom was still listed as the majority owner of the company and no criminal involvement could be traced to her.

Things were developing at a rapid pace and the Hoodfellas had . better put their foot down to keep the bloodshed to a minimum. Deon knew he had to get rid of Giuseppe in order to send a strong message to the mob. Since the Dog Pound Posse had done a good job to get rid of the three mob associates, Deon decided to hire them to get rid of all the associates. A sum of two million was agreed upon and the Dog Pound Posse promised they would wipe out the associates. Giuseppe, however, was a personal task that Deon felt he had to take care himself. Cindy had never worked the front desk; she was always in the back in her private office, so she was the perfect bait. She worked behind the scenes as a publicist for the company. Giuseppe never connected her to the Luxurious Life, LLC. However, Giuseppe's mob hangout wasn't hard to find. Cindy was breathtaking in every way to most white men, and Giuseppe's Achilles heel was his affinity for beautiful women.

After describing the red-headed Italian bad boy to Cindy, Deon told her to make sure she gets him back to her hotel, so he could finish the job. The isolated Marriott in midtown Miami was the perfect setting. Cindy was one of few women in the Italian bar owned by the mob boss when she arrived there. She wore a hot, eye-catching outfit that sent the boys to their knees. The fishnet pantyhose, high heels, and short black dress were enough to get Giuseppe to start flexing his muscle to let her know his status as a made man. He assumed she was from the neighborhood and was aware of the mob hangout. "What brought you to our beautiful place today?" Giuseppe asked as he approached her. New pussy could always get a man in trouble. "Can't a girl just have a drink in peace?" she told him while she tried to get the attention of the bartender. "You must be new in town cause I ain't never seen your face here before. Are you some kind of cop or something?" Giuseppe asked suspiciously. "You must have something to hide if you're worried about me being a cop. But to satisfy your curiosity, I'm not a cop. I'm just a girl looking to get a little work so I can pay a few bills," Cindy told him. "What would you like to drink, Miss?" the bartender asked. "I'll have an Amaretto sour on the rocks," she told him as she reached into her purse to get the money to pay for it. "Your money's no good here. I got it," Giuseppe told her. "Thank you," she told him. "So how can a guy like me have a good time with a woman like you?" he asked. To put his mind at ease, she told him she charged five hundred dollars an hour and she would do anything he wanted.

Confident that Cindy was not a cop, Giuseppe asked, "How about my boys, can they get in on the action as well?" Cindy looked over to the three Italian men standing near the pool table gawking at her and said, "I ain't into gangbanging, but as long as they can each afford five hundred dollars an hour, they can get my services, too." Giuseppe smiled and went over to his boys to tell them the good news. The four of them decided to follow Cindy to the Marriott. Giuseppe agreed to go first while two of the guys stayed in the car and another stood guard by the door upstairs outside the room. Cindy was willing to do whatever it took for the team, and if letting Giuseppe fuck her was part of it to get the other guard away from the door, so be it. No one wants to stand guard near a door while a woman is screaming at the top of her lungs in ecstasy, anyway. She was about to put on the best performance these boys.

Crusher was pissed and ready to kill somebody because the sweet girl that he once knew was murdered. Somebody was going to pay the price for her death. The beautiful stars in the sky set a peaceful and worry free atmosphere for the two mobsters sitting in the black Cadillac Deville in the parking lot of the hotel. The two of them were discussing what they were going to do to Cindy. Their excitement was heightened after the man who stood guard by the door called them on their cellphone to report that Cindy was a screaming freak and he couldn't wait to get his turn. While engaged in a conversation with each other about the upcoming sexual romp, the two mobsters let their guard down. They didn't even see Smitty and Evelyne in the shadows. By the time they realized they had been had, Smitty and Evelyne were letting off shots into their bodies as the silencers on the guns muffled the sounds. The guard outside the door moved down the hallway, away from the screaming Cindy in the room, but he wanted to keep the two men in the car updated. After calling the cellphones of the two men and he got no answer, he became worried. He wanted to go and check on them to make sure everything was fine. He opted for the back stairs instead of the elevator.

His destination was death no matter which way he chose to go. Deon and Mean T were waiting in each of the two elevators with guns in hand, so they could blast him. From the stairway, Crusher kept his eyes on the bodyguard the whole time he was in the hallway. After taking a step behind the door to go down the steps to check on his men, he was shot point blank in the back of the head. Crusher lost it and unloaded a full clip on him. The bullet-riddled body of the bodyguard flung down the steps like a rag doll. Crusher placed a call to Deon to let him know that the bodyguard had been taken care of. Smitty had also placed a call to Deon about fifteen minutes earlier after completing his task along with Evelyne. Deon and Mean T moved upstairs to check on Cindy. All was silent as Deon knocked on the door to check on Cindy. Giuseppe didn't even get a chance to taste Cindy's pussy. One of Giuseppe's favorite pastimes was receiving blowjobs from women. While Cindy's lips were wrapped around his dick and her tongue doing magical curls around it, Giuseppe closed his eyes while moaning to enjoy the feeling. He never once saw her reach under the pillow to pull out the baby 9mm handgun to blow his head off. She continued screaming as if he was banging the hell out of her to keep the bodyguard from becoming suspicious. The bodyguard behind the door was fooled. When Cindy finally opened the door to let Deon in, he found Giuseppe's body in a pool of blood. Tony pulled out an army knife and chopped Giuseppe's head off his body. He took the head and wrapped it in the plastic laundry bag that was hanging in the closet and then wrapped it in a couple of pillow cases before leaving the bloody room.

The situation soon turned to sadness when Deon, Tony, Crusher and Cindy arrived downstairs to find Evelyne's dead body in Smitty's arms. "What the fuck happened!" Deon yelled. "Man, we thought we took out both of the men, but the one Evelyne shot wasn't completely dead, and as we were walking away, he shot her in her face before I finished him off. I'm sorry, man," Smitty told them. Just like that, Evelyne's dream of a better life in America was cut short by a bullet as well. She was definitely down for the crew and she would do anything for them. Her dream was to settle down with Crusher and have a bunch of babies some day.

Another Funeral

Plans for the funeral and burial of Rosie and Maribel had been set, but unfortunately Evelyne had to be added to the list. Deon couldn't believe how he was losing everyone around him so quickly. It just seemed like everything he had done was coming back to haunt him. Deon's plan to retire a wealthy businessman was slipping away and he was starting to lose confidence from the surviving members of his team. Crusher suggested they close up shop because the bloodshed seemed endless and they wouldn't have time to enjoy the money they fought so hard to obtain. "Man, this is like four bodies in the last couple of weeks. I don't know if I can stand to lose another member of the crew. Me, you and Cindy are the only original members that are left from the crew, man. We've been fighting ever since we came outta prison. When is it gonna stop? You know I ain't no punk, but man, I'm tired of this street war shit. I just wanna lay back and chill for the remainder of my days on this earth," Crusher told Deon sadly. Deon shook his head and understood exactly where Crusher was coming from. "We here planning funerals after funerals and we don't even know who's next. It ain't like they ain't gonna come back to take one of us out because of what we did to their men. I've been fighting for too long. I think we should get rid of the business, split the money and go live the rest of our lives in obscurity," he suggested. Deon took a long look at him and said, "Are we runners now? I didn't know you to ever run from anybody. We gotta give these bastards all that we've got, and I'm ready to die to do that. If you ain't with me, I can understand that, but I'm gonna fight. They ain't running me out!" Deon said firmly.

Crusher pondered Deon's words for a minute before walking away to go view Evelyne's body. He had lost the woman he wanted to spend the rest of his life with and saw no way out of a life he no longer wanted to live. Crusher had been fighting since he was a teenager and the fighting went on during most of his prison sentence. As much as he was a dedicated soldier to Deon, Crusher contemplated a new life with a wife and children. However, he came to the realization that perhaps that was not in the cards for him. He walked back to Deon after viewing Evelyne's body in the coffin and said, "We're gonna kill each and every single one of them bastards!" Deon smiled and hugged his friend like they needed each other more than ever. Though Deon was the leader of the crew, he knew he needed the support and back of his best friend in order to survive the game.

The bodies of Rosie, Maribel and Evelyne lay peacefully in their coffins, as the remaining members of the Hoodfellas reflected on the short memories they shared with them. Crusher was especially disturbed by their deaths because Evelyne had become his woman and he was also fond of Rosie as a friend. Maribel was the hot Spanish chica who taught the crew the little Spanish they had learned. Deon and Cindy were sad over the death of Maribel because the three of them were in an unofficial relationship. He vowed revenge for her. All the happiness that Deon and his crew thought money would bring to them, never came. The funeral was only attended by the Hoddfellas family. It was then that Deon realized it was them against the world. There was no extended family to rely on. Tony and Serena played the role of parents by trying to comfort them, but how can you comfort somebody who just lost three members of his family?

One of the things Deon was not accustomed to was tears, and it wasn't going to start with the deaths of Rosie, Maribel and Evelyne. He was a leader and he needed to be strong in order to continue on with the war. He looked around and only noticed three standing soldiers left from his crew. He wanted to make sure they were protected. He didn't want to see them in a box. He would rather die first before Cindy, Smitty and Cusher were killed. There was complete silence in the stretched limousine that drove them from the church to the cemetery. Even Smitty wasn't his usual hyper self, always ready to take on the world. At that moment, silence was golden. The crew knew exactly what they needed to do in order to beat the mob at their own game.

Message To The Mob

Giuseppe's decapitated head was specially delivered to the mob hangout spot in South Florida. Smitty was assigned the duty of delivering the severed head to the front door of the mob while riding a Ninja motorcycle. Shots rang out as Smitty rode by with a machine gun and sprayed the place after tossing Giuseppe's head towards the front door. The gangsters inside ducked for cover as they heard the philharmonic sounds of bullets ringing a dangerous tune through the front door and windows. No one got a glimpse of the man wearing a black ski mask, as he sped away on the black sport bike. Only streaks of burning rubber and smoke were left as he disappeared into oblivion. By the time the mobsters got to open the bag containing Giuseppe's head, words like "Those fucking niggers are gonna pay!" were flying all over the place. They were mad that a group of black men had the nerve to test their limits with them. The incident went from the Capo all the way up to the Don. It would be taken care of, once and for all, they believed.

While the mob was thinking that they had to teach the Hoodfellas a lesson, Deon was sending a message of his own: <u>His crew had guns, too, and they were gonna keep killing until there was no one left standing.</u> How do you deal with a man who's ready to die? The mob was about to find out that death was the least of Deon's worries. A couple of days after Giuseppe's head was thrown through the front door of the bar, Deon showed up with two machine guns in his hands, wearing army fatigues and carrying enough grenades to take out a village. The mob hangout was no more after Deon walked out. Everyone inside dove for cover as Deon unloaded two full clips of ammunition while standing in the middle of the bar. After walking out, he tossed two grenades inside to ensure the decimation of every mob member inside.

Deon gave the mob very little time to think about his mental state. His insanity was incomprehensible. Not even his crew knew of his antics. Deon had made the decision to deal with the mob in the most insane way. He wanted to take the war to their doorstep and he didn't care about the consequences. No one made it out the bar to tell about the lone gunman who came in and destroyed the place. Deon became a figment of everybody's imagination. Not even the mob boss could believe what happened. However, the message was clear to him that he was dealing with a demented Negro.

Newscasters were speechless as they scrambled to report on the explosion that took place at the well-known secretive mob hangout. Most people speculated the explosion was related to mob crimes. Even the cops were baffled because the place had been under surveillance by the Federal Bureau of Investigation for a long time. Not even the two agents stationed about a block away from the bar saw Deon go in the bar. The agents only knew something had happened went the place blew up in smithereens and debris from the explosion hit their window. The knee-jerk reaction by them to duck for cover gave Deon just enough time to make his way down the street on the bike parked behind the bar.

Deon had been casing the joint and he knew the emergency exit was the best way to surprise the goons inside. He had been watching the agents across the street for weeks, even before he sent Cindy to the bar while wearing a blonde wig to get Giuseppe back to her hotel room. When he wanted Smitty to deliver Giuseppe's head to the mob, he paid a couple guys handsomely to create a diversion that would pull the two FBI agents from their post. The two arguing men started fighting in plain view of the agents, which gave Smitty enough time to accomplish his mission. Deon wanted to show the mob that not even the FBI was a deterrent enough to keep his crew from attacking them. He got that message across loud and clear.

Mean T aka Abdul aka Tony

Mean T sat back as he watched Deon handle things in an expeditious manner. He was proud of what he saw and he knew that Deon had always had leadership qualities. He stayed in the background during the war with the mob, because he couldn't afford to serve another prison term. It was hard enough that he served his entire sentence to avoid being on parole, but he was not looking forward to a second stint in prison. He definitely didn't want to risk his freedom again. However, he was more than willing to stand with Deon even if his life depended on it. This time, he would go out in a blaze of glory.

Mean T had served time in prison since he was a teenager, and all those years behind bars gave him the affordability to learn and read about many different things in life, including the mob. He was the educator as well as the reference guide for Deon as it related to the mob. He explained the structural component of the mob to Deon and told him what he may be possibly up against. Taking out the Capo was just the beginning of an endless war and Deon didn't have the fire power or the soldiers to withstand a long battle. Guerilla warfare was his best weapon and he had better learn to use it in order to stand a chance. In case a truce was on the horizon, Mean T wanted to make himself available as the negotiator, but they had already gone too far and exhausted all chances for a truce. While Deon was out to win the war, the mobsters were also setting up their own strategy to emerge victorious. After the big bombing, everyone was on edge. It became a chess game and paranoia started to set in on both sides.

The mob boss or the don, Salvatore Mancini ordered his underboss, Francesco Mancini, to wipe out the Hoodfellas. Mean T already knew that the next move from the mob would come from the top and he advised Deon to step up security at the mansion. Francesco would stop at nothing to prove to his father and boss that he was capable of pulling the biggest job ever assigned to him. The Luxurious Life LLC's business office was closed while the investigation into the death of Maribel and Rosie was ongoing. The Hoodfellas' place of business was no longer a target as no one was there to be killed by the mob. The next focus was their residence. Though the Hoodfellas lived in a highly secured gated community on Star Island, Mean T knew that the mob could always find a way to breach security.   The three full-time armed security guards who worked at the front gate were known to Deon and his crew, and Deon always went out of his way to make sure they all earned an extra thousand dollars a week for providing extra security to his property. The money the security guards were earning under the table from the Hoodfellas surpassed their weekly salaries. Their loyalty was to the Hoodfellas and Deon knew he could trust them.

While the security team was bought and paid for, Mean T wasn't so confident that the mob wouldn't be able to find a way in. He urged Deon to install more surveillance cameras to capture every single inch of the house from every angle and to also install a laser alarm that would trigger an invasion from intruders. Safety was of the utmost importance as the Hoodfellas became prisoners in their own homes. Though some of them didn't want to heed Mean T's warnings and thought that the mob would back down, Crusher and Smitty unfortunately found out the hard way.

It's Been A Long Time

Through all the turmoil going on, Serena and Tony were just getting acquainted. There was no anticipation on Tony's part. Tony was as patient as he had ever been since he came home from prison. Sex was no longer the primary thing on Tony's mind after he laid eyes on Serena. He was too old to be looking for a fling, so he set his mind on winning her heart. The two of them spent as much time enjoying the little things that most people take for granted. Having spent so much time in prison shaped their views of life. Bird-watching was one of their favorite things as it was considered a pastime in prison. They both dreamed about being free as a bird one day, and now it was a reality. They had also forgone their youth due to incarceration, so now it was time for the two lovebirds to act like teenagers again. Serena and Tony became inseparable and they enjoyed spending every moment with each other. Of course, reminiscing about old times was one of their favorite things. They talked about how crazy Sticky Fingers was and how Deon looked so much like him. The two of them also went on long walks, watched movies together and spent time getting reacquainted with each other.

Skipping rocks over the water at the beach and feeding the birds suddenly had more meaning to Serena and Tony. Courting Serena was something new for Tony. He had never gone after a woman before. The two of them hadn't been intimate with anybody in over twenty years. At first, it was a little awkward for Tony to get his groove in motion. He didn't really know what to do. He didn't want to move too fast, because he didn't want to offend Serena. He was trying to allow nature to take its course. One night while they were taking a stroll at the private beach located in their complex, Tony held on to Serena's hand and started smiling as he gazed into her eyes. His feeling was reciprocated when Serena pulled him closer for a passionate kiss. The kiss seemed endless as Tony slowly took Serena's tongue in his mouth and caressed it with ease and almost didn't want to stop to breathe. Serena was a little surprised that Tony kissed so well. Perhaps it was just the fact that the two of them were into each other.

The moon-lit night provided the perfect opportunity for Tony and Serena to explore the splendor of the private beach, alone. The breeze coming from afar felt heavenly against their hot bodies. After serving thirty years in prison,

Tony had the body of a professional bodybuilder. Serena felt the contours of his chiseled chest and his huge biceps and became a little moister than she anticipated. She was feeling horny for the first time in a long time. She wondered if Tony felt the same way. She didn't have to wonder too long after laying eyes on the huge bulge in Tony's pants. He wanted her. She wanted him. Somebody had to make that move. However, it was a lot easier for Serena to find the evidential signs that Tony wanted her through his pants. Tony on the other was a little clueless. He didn't want to disrespect Serena by shoving his hand down her panties to check for moisture. The loose white linen mini dress Serena was sporting easily gave Tony access to her fountain of youth, but he was not sure whether his adolescent cravings would be fulfilled.

Tony had no idea that Serena had her own agenda. The palm tree standing near the water not only provided back support, but it also provided a little bit of obscurity from view in case a Peeping Tom was lurking. Serena took the opportunity to pin Tony against the tree so she could allow her tongue a voyage up and down his body. After unbuttoning his shirt, Serena slowly started to leave a wet kiss trail across his chest. Tony was pleasantly surprised by Serena's sudden aggression. He was elated! As her tongue twirled across his chest and down near his navel, Tony almost had a quick embarrassing moment. However, he held back and continued to enjoy Serena's tongue massage. As she reached to unfasten his belt, he spread his legs apart for comfort and allowed his ten-inch dick to spill freely out of his underwear and into Serena's mouth. He reached back to hold on to the tree as Serena savored a good six inches of his dick in her mouth. The warmth of her mouth sent chills up and down his spine. Serena thought his dick was just delicious as she licked it over and over and over again.

Meanwhile, Tony couldn't help his own curiosity as he reached down to feel the moisture between Serena's thighs. He stuck a finger in her pussy and then took it to his mouth. She tasted good. Now, it was her turn to get pinned against the tree as he pulled up her dress to have an oral journey of his own with her pussy. Not the expert that Serena expected with his tongue, she decided to help him with his course. "Slow with the tongue, baby," she instructed him. Tony's pussy eating debut was not great, but with the help of Serena, he managed. "Yes, keep your tongue on my clit, baby, and lick it slowly. Right there! Oh yes! Oh shit! Don't stop! Eat my pussy, baby!" Serena instructed. Feeling a little more confident with his rhythm, Tony pulled back the foreskin over Serena's clit and started rubbing it with his finger while he tongue fucked her. She decided to let go of the tree and grabbed his bald head for comfort instead. Serena was chasing her own nut as she held on tight to Tony's head to wind over his mouth. Moments later, she was in a trance and Tony had accomplished the mission of forcing an orgasm out of Serena.

Serena may have been older, but her beautiful body remained. Her ass was as plumped and round as it had ever been and Tony got a full view of it when she turned around and stuck it out to him while holding on to the tree. It was as if Serena was expecting a voracious Tony to plow her pussy, as she braced herself for it. Tony, however, was a lot gentler than she expected. His massive build could easily be misconstrued for roughness, but Tony was a gentle lover. He slowly penetrated Serena and built up a slow tempo that she found soothing. As his dick filled her pussy, Serena's secretion started pouring all over his dick. Her eyes stayed closed as his heavenly strokes took her to paradise. She couldn't believe how good it felt to make love. Tony straightened her body up so he could get a little closer to her. He held her body tight as he stroked a nut into her. "Yes baby! Here it comes," he murmured to her. Tony held up her right leg to push his entire dick inside. Serena's bouncy ass just added to the ecstatic feeling of a long awaited nut that

Tony wanted to experience with her. "Oh shit! I'm cumin baby!" he exclaimed as his semen invaded her pussy. Though the two of them seemed exhausted, after a five minute retreat, they went at it again and again until they were ready to go back to the house to go to sleep.

Serena and Tony were in love. For the next few weeks, they took care of each other and made plans to live the rest of their lives together. With the success of Deon's business, they didn't have any more financial worries, as he provided for both of them. Serena's plan was to teach Tony everything he needed to know to be the best lover, friend and homey to her. It was inevitable that they started falling in love with each other.

The Mob Strikes Back?

Crusher had started to become addicted to Popeye's chicken since his return to the States. There was no substitute for his cravings of the Louisiana original recipe. His voracious appetite for chicken had also been substituting the lost of Evelyne. He was eating more than usual as he mourned her death. He especially liked the breast part of the chicken and there was nothing that could keep him from going out to get his chicken. It was late in the evening when Crusher decided to hop in the Range Rover to drive about five miles to Biscayne Boulevard to buy a bucket of his favorite fried chicken. His mouth was watering as he thought about the succulent, Cajun flavored, spicy pieces of crisp chicken being slowly masticated in his mouth, so he could savor the taste. "Man, I know T advised us not to expose ourselves in the street, but I gotta get some chicken," he said to Smitty while the two of them were in the game room playing pool. "Man, shit, I can definitely use some of that Popeye's chicken right about now. I'll roll with ya," Smitty told him. "Yo, let me just tell D we're rolling out. I was a prisoner for almost twenty years of my life when I was locked up; I ain't gonna let nobody hold me captive in my own home. The mob can come get some of this if they want to," he said as he pulled out two automatic handguns, raised them and then placed them around his waist on his back. "Well, they gonna have to take me out with you," Smitty said as he showed off his own loaded guns, ready to take out an army if need be.

Crusher went upstairs to tell Deon of his plans to go buy some chicken from Popeye's. "You're a grown ass man. You can do whatever you want to do, but just be careful. I need my best general beside me in case I have to go to war," Deon playfully told him. "You already know how it is. Dem boys ain't ready for us," Crusher said as he grabbed the keys to the Range to head out. "Just remember, we have to be ready for them!" Deon shouted back as Crusher made his way out the door.

By this time, Deon trusted no one but his immediate Hoodfellas family. He didn't want anybody near him or them. While Crusher and Smitty were on their way to Popeye's, Deon got a visit from a visitor he wasn't expecting that late at night. "We have a delivery for Mr. Campbell," the Asian man told the security guard at the front gate. "I will take it to Mr. Campbell for you," the security guard suggested while he pulled out a pen to sign for the package. However, it wasn't that kind of package. The cooler sitting in the back seat of the Asian man's 3-series BMW looked suspicious to the security guard. He immediately unfastened the clasp to the holster of his weapon while keeping his finger on the trigger. "This is a special delivery and I need to personally make sure it gets delivered to Mr. Campbell," the Asian man reiterated firmly. "Ok, so we gonna play this game where I tell you that you can't go to Mr. Campbell's house, and you're gonna keep repeating that you have to go, right? Ain't gonna happen, buddy," the security guard assured. "Well, call Mr. Campbell and tell him that there's a special delivery here for him from Tommy Li in Boston," the Asian man kindly suggested. "How about I ain't gonna call Mr. Campbell, because he told me not to let anybody in to see him, and you're gonna turn your little Asian ass around before I put a cap in your ass," the security guard said as he pulled his weapon out.

Unbeknownst to the security guard, his revolver was only a weapon against himself when he faced the Asian man. The Asian man reached out the driver's window and disarmed the security guard so fast, he didn't even see what happened. "Please don't kill me!" he begged. The Asian man's motive was never to kill the security guard. He ordered him to open the gate, took directions to Deon's house from the guard and then made his way into the complex. The guard quickly called Deon on the phone as the Asian man took off towards his house. "Mr. Campbell! There's an Asian man coming to your house talking about he got some special delivery for you from Boston. I tried to stop him, but he was lightning fast. Be careful, 'cause he sneaky and fast and shit!" the security guard reported. Deon didn't have to ask any questions as he started to smile to himself. He knew it was one of Tommy's Li's people. "Everything will be fine. I know who it is," Deon assured the security guard. "You know if you need me Mr. Campbell, I'm just a phone call away. I'll bring my shotgun since he took my handgun," the guard told Deon in a shaken voice. "Don't worry about it. It's all good," Deon reassured him.

Though Deon hadn't anticipated Tommy Li's associate, he was happy that the heads of Case and his men were delivered to him on ice as he requested. The Asian man drove straight from Boston to deliver the heads to Deon as agreed. Deon handed him a bag, which contained the balance of the money. Their conversation was brief as the man left to get back on the road to Boston. That encounter also reminded Deon that he had options against the mob. He was now considering hiring the Chinese Connection to help assist him against the mob. Deon also took the decapitated heads and placed them in a cooler.

The security guard spotted the headlights of the BMW right away as it sped towards the gate. He tried to mean mug the Asian man, but the Asian man only smiled as he tossed the Security guard's gun back to him before exiting the gate. "That mu'fucker had better gave me back my gun or that would've been his ass," the security guard mumbled to himself after the Asian man was out of sight.

About ten minutes later, a frantic Smitty pulled up to the gate with Crusher hunched over in the passenger seat in a pool of blood. "Open the fucking gate!" he screamed to the security before the security guard got a chance to make small talk with him. The security guard had been trying to get down with the Hoodfellas since they moved into the complex. He had no idea about their illegal dealings. He only knew about the Luxurious Life, LLC, and that was enough for him to want to be down. Smitty shielded Crusher's blood-soaked body from the security guard as he sped away to the house. After pulling into the garage, he screamed for Deon to come help him, "Help me! Help Me!" Deon and Tony grabbed their guns and ran towards the garage to see what the commotion was all about. "What the fuck is going on?" Deon asked. "They shot him, D. We got ambushed. We didn't even see them pull up on us," Smiity said through sobs. "Damn!" Deon said as he banged his fist against the wall. "Maybe he's still alive. Let me check him," said Tony. All hopes were gone as Tony felt for a pulse and found none. "Who the fuck did this?" Deon asked angrily. "Those fucking Guido motherfuckers! I took a couple of them out, but there was too many of them. I had to get out of dodge," Smitty told them. Both sides of the Range Rover were bullet riddled. Deon was pissed and he had to go back and exact revenge while his blood was still boiling hot. It was one more death that Deon wasn't expecting.

It's Time For War!

Deon was riled up as he told his troops to grab their guns, because he was ready for war. Unfortunately, there weren't that many troops left. As Deon looked around, his crew had decimated to five people, and that included his "Ride or Die" mother. He knew he didn't have a hold on the situation, but something had to be done about all those deaths that his crew suffered. Even the general manager of the Luxurious Life, LLC had quit on him. He called Deon to resign his position after Maribel and Rosie were shot dead in front of the office. Deon's world was crumbling and he refused to lay down his guns. However, not everybody was willing to die a hero with him. "Look D, you're battling a winless battle. There's no way to continue with this shit without having more casualties. I appreciate what you've done for me, but I think it's about time you take a new direction and leave this war well enough alone. I've never been a coward in my entire life, but I always used good judgment to fight my battles. I say we pack our shit and leave this town once and for all. It's not like you ain't got enough money to live in obscurity for the rest of your life. Fuck the Luxurious Life, LLC. Just go somewhere and have yourself some kids with your girl and chill," Tony told him. Deon had a devilish look on his face after listening to Tony's soliloquy. "You're fucking bailing out on me now after all I've done for you?" he screamed at Tony. Deon was allowing his ego to get in the way of his thought process. He would've never made it out of prison alive without Tony. Perhaps the millions of dollars that he had earned since coming out of prison had erased his memory, but Tony was man enough to let him vent. "I built this shit and ain't nobody gonna take it from me or run me out of town!" Deon exclaimed.

The room was silent for a while as Deon's insanity took a Tony Montana turn. "I'll kill every single one of those sons of bitches. I ain't going nowhere! These motherfuckers ain't seen the last of me!" he proclaimed. Everyone was baffled and confused. They didn't understand what Deon wanted from them. No one dared to talk because they didn't want the wrath of Deon to come down on them, well, except for one person. "Look, I know you're young, ambitious and angry, son, but you can't lose yourself by allowing a situation to control you. If you close up shop, the mob loses. What the fuck are they gonna collect? And who they gonna kill? We ain't gonna be here for them to kill us. We can still go somewhere else and live in peace. Anyway, I don't know about you, but me and your mother were thinking about moving to a small town in South Carolina. We're too old for this shit. We want to live the rest of our lives in peace," Tony told him. "Oh now you're speaking for my mother, too? You're gonna go with him? It don't matter no way. It ain't like you've ever been there for me my whole life anyway. Go ahead take your ass to South Carolina with him. I don't need none of y'all!" Deon told them in anger.

As cool as Deon had been since he came out of prison, this was the first time that he had shown weakness in his leadership. Maybe the death of his whole crew drove him insane and he didn't know any other way to cope. The sweet life that Deon had dreamed about for his crew never came about, because he couldn't control the different elements in the world. Perhaps it was karma that was causing all those things to happen in his life, but Deon was about to bust under pressure and he really had no idea what to do to get the results he wanted. Any suggestion or advice he received fell on deaf ears, because the thing he wanted the most was his long gone crew that he couldn't bring back.

"Don't worry, D, I'm down with you 'til the end," Smitty told him. "Me too, baby," Cindy chimed in. "See, that's what I'm talking about. Real soldiers don't run away from a fight. We're gonna give these motherfuckers a fight they never saw coming," Deon announced. "Deon, you're my only son and I've missed so much time away from you. I don't want to see you in a box before it's your time. Why don't you just listen to Tony and leave this place? It's not like you need the money. What you got to prove? You're the only family I've got left. As much as I love you, I think you're making the wrong decision. Too many people have died already. I really think you ought to think about this more," Serena said while tears dropped from her eyes. Still, Deon was not connecting to anybody's emotions but his own. He couldn't understand why they wanted to walk away from the situation. His mother was the first person to tell him that he had to be ready to die for his achievements. Tony said the same thing to him and he started to believe it. In a way, Deon found it hypocritical that they were running when the threat was imminent.

When Serena moved to Florida, Deon had given her a million dollars, which she kept in a duffle bag. She wanted to use the money to start over with Tony, but she still wanted to make sure her son was going to be okay. It broke her heart that he didn't want to listen to anybody, but he was a grown man, making a decision that affected his life. With sadness in her voice, Serena said goodbye to her son and told him that she loved him, while giving him a less receptive hug. "You make sure you take care of yourself, D. I appreciate all that you've done for me since I moved down here, but I didn't come home from prison to die on the streets. I will always love you like a son, but your mother and I need to live life a little. We spent most of our lives in peril, it's about time that we enjoy life a little," Tony told him while trying to hug a standoffish Deon. "I ain't worried about y'all. And y'all ain't got to worry about me!" Deon told them before they walked out to the waiting cab to take them to the train station. "I love you, son," his mother tearfully uttered before closing the door behind her.

If Deon was ready for war, he realized he had to do it with Cindy and Smitty only. He knew it was a suicidal mission. He decided that he would buy himself the manpower needed to eliminate the mob. "I'm gonna take care of this!" he declared as he pulled his cellphone to place a call to Tommy Li. "Hey Tommy," he said on the receiver after Tommy picked up the phone on the second ring. "I appreciate the special delivery," he said referring to the decapitated heads using coded language on the phone. "I have a new gig paying about five mil. I wanted to know if you're interested," he told Tommy. "You're an interesting man, Deon. I like you because you keep me employed. What's this new gig entail?" Tommy asked. "I'll be on the first plane tomorrow morning to discuss it with you," Deon told him before hanging up the phone.

Tommy Li

As promised, Deon boarded an early flight to Boston to go meet with Tommy Li about his new business proposal. Tommy had always been there to provide the extra muscle for the Hoodfellas whenever Deon needed him. While on the plane, Deon's face was filled with anger. He was cold to the flight attendant and he made it known to the guy sitting next to him in first class that he didn't want to be bothered. All he could think about was the annihilation of his enemy to remove the threat that surrounded him. He left special instructions for Cindy and Smitty to stay in the house for their own safety, after they dropped him off at the airport. Deon was always a thinking man, but he seemed like he was losing his edge because he had allowed his problems to take a toll on him emotionally. The cool-headed Deon was no longer. Insanity can be triggered by the smallest event, but Deon's insanity seemed justified because the family he had known and loved for most of his life had been taken away from him. Anger was now his only outlet and vengeance seemed to be the only suitable therapy to cure his insanity.

He had it all planned in his head when he deplaned to catch a waiting limousine to take him to Chinatown for his meeting with Tommy Li. Deon thought the Chinese Connection had the answer to his problem and he felt relief was coming soon. It took about ten minutes for the limo driver to get to Chinatown from Logan airport. Deon was greeted once again by Tommy Li's assistant, Rachel Ling, but this time their encounter was more cordial. Rachel remembered Deon right away. He had become a special client with high status to the Chinese Connection. There was no problem for Rachel to escort him to the waiting Tommy Li in his office.

The two men hugged instantly after they saw each other. "It's nice to see you again, Deon," Tommy said to him. Deon was anxious, so he didn't really seem to be in the mood for small talk, but he had to show respect. "It's always good to see you, but I want to get down straight to business. I need a whole bunch of motherfuckers dead and I don't care what it takes," Deon told him. "I've never seen you so emotional. Relax, man. I'm sure we can take care of it," Tommy assured him before Deon even said anything to him about his arch enemy. "Man, these motherfuckers wiped out half my crew and I need to make sure I wipe out their entire crew," Deon sounded pissed. "Who are we dealing with this time?" Tommy asked in a calm voice while slowly pacing back and forth in his office like a sensei. "Man, these motherfucking Guidos in Miami think they can force my hand. They're about to feel my wrath. Ain't nobody gonna be left alive!" Deon said as he pounded his fist into his hand. "I assume you're talking about the mob, right?" Tommy asked. "Yeah. Dem assholes have killed all my people. I need them wiped out like yesterday. Fucking Mancini family think they're untouchable," Deon said in anger. "Did you say Mancini family?" Tommy asked for confirmation. "Yeah, is there a problem?" Deon asked with curiosity. "Deon, I'm afraid I'm not gonna be able to take that job," Tommy told him disappointingly. "Why not?" Deon asked baffled. "Look, I would advise you to pack your shit and get outta town while you can, my friend. You don't wanna fuck with the Mancini Borgata. I thought you met with them from the very beginning when you decided to open your business in Miami," Tommy said with a nod of surprise. "Why would I fucking meet with them before starting my business, are they the fucking licensing board in Miami?" Deon said sarcastically. The two men were obviously on different pages and Tommy was trying to be as diplomatic as possible to let Deon know he didn't stand a chance against the Mancini family.

"I guess you haven't done your homework, or you didn't do your homework this time. The Mancini Borgata is the most ruthless mob family to ever hit Miami. These men are calculated and murderous in the worse way. They don't care about your men, they want you. They always go all the way to the top to make an example out of the leaders in case some of the soldiers think they can stand the heat. This family has the mayor in their pocket, the judges, cops, politicians and sometimes even the district attorney. As your friend, I would advise you to count your losses and keep it moving, fast!" Tommy told him. "Oh now you're punking out, too. Man fuck the Mancini family, they're about to meet the Hoodfellas family and we're gonna bring it to them!" Deon said angrily. Tommy just shook his head and said, "So you're gonna hire some street thugs to go against an organized crime family and you think you're gonna win? Don't be a statistic to the game, Deon. Every game has its rules and you can't always try to bend the rules your way. I'm sorry I won't be able to help, but good luck with everything, my friend," Tommy told him before escorting him to the door to hop back in his waiting limousine to go back to airport.

Another Surprise

Deon's meeting with the Chinese Connection didn't go according to plan, and his stubbornness continued to get in the way of his sanity. After arriving back at the airport, he caught the first plane back to Miami. Normally, Deon would fly a private plane, but he wasn't willing to wait for the private plane to be serviced, so he flew commercial. While on the plane, Deon couldn't understand how the Mancini family could be so intimidating, even to the Chinese Connection. How could an illegal entity be so powerful? He wondered. This was the kind of power he yearned for. He wanted people to respect and fear him. He had always wanted his reputation to precede him. Deon felt the only way to do that was to stand up against the mob. He didn't have too much time to strategize because Tommy had warned that they were probably going to be gunning for him. Deon never feared death, because he had escaped it so many times. However, his nonchalant attitude about the situation was about to change.

Smitty and Cindy picked up Deon from the airport as planned, and they went straight to the house. Deon was miserable and there was nothing that Cindy or Smitty could do to help ease his mind. He asked Cindy to go in the kitchen to get him a glass of water. Smitty also followed behind Cindy acting as if he was going to his room to look for something in his room. Moments later, Deon heard a single gunshot coming from the kitchen. Before he could get up from the couch to check what's going on in the kitchen, Smitty emerged with two guns drawn on Deon. He thought maybe he was hallucinating. "Where's Cindy?" Deon asked, thinking that Smitty had drawn his gun because he heard gunshots. "That bitch is dead with a single bullet to her head. It was so easy. Now it's your turn to die," Smitty told him. "I ain't got time for your stupid jokes and I ain't in the mood for it," Deon told Smitty firmly. "This ain't a joke, bro," Smitty told him as he fired a shot into Deon's arm. The reality of the situation finally hit Deon when he jumped behind the couch for cover. "You just think you're invincible, huh?" Smitty started a soliloquy. "You thought you could take my father out and get away with it, huh? Well, today is judgment day and you can say goodbye to your maker," Smitty said as he unleashed a barrage of shots into the couch. Deon pulled out his own weapon and started returing fire blindly across the room. "You little fucking ingrate. Who the fuck is your father?" Deon asked as he unleashed a few shots of his own. "My father's name was Wally, but I never got to know him because you and your men killed him. I'm about to kill you and take all your shit just like you did him," Smitty said in a deadly tone while unloading a clip towards the couch. Deon was obviously hit and blood was splattered all across the floor.

Smitty's murderous rage became a confession as he started to reveal in detail how he had shot Mike, Evelyne, Crusher and now Cindy. "You thought you had some real soldiers, willing and ready to die for your cause. Well, I ain't a soldier. My father was a general and I have general blood. I'm gonna kill you for never giving me a chance to have my father in my life. You about to die, bitch!" Smitty exclaimed as he approached the couch to finish Deon off. One single shot was heard in the quiet moment, and it didn't come from Deon or Smitty's gun. The shot went straight to the back of Smitty's head. Smitty was dead on impact.

Smitty didn't even hear Serena making her way through the house with her baby 9mm in hand and Tony behind her with two 9mm handguns in hand. Serena knew something was going on when she and Tony pulled up in front of the house and heard gunshots after exiting the cab.

Tony had been paying close attention to all the people who had gotten shot whenever they went out with Smitty. It was odd that he kept coming back to the house with another person on his watch always dying. Tony grew suspicious, but what finally caught his attention was the way that Crusher was killed. It took him a while to think about it, but Crusher was shot on the left side of his head. When Smitty came to the house, he claimed he was driving, so the only way Crusher could've been shot was by the driver. Serena helped Tony put the pieces together when she recalled how much Smitty looked like this man named Wally Webster who left her disfigured many years ago. He was a carbon copy of his father in every way and it was kind of eerie to Serena. She couldn't pinpoint it at first, but after Tony's suspicion grew, she was able to connect the dots and realized that Smitty was out for revenge against her son. Deon had told Serena about killing Wally and his men took away all his money.

The mob killing of Maribel and Rosie was very different from the way the rest of the Hoodfellas had been taken out. Serena and Tony decided to make a detour when they realized Deon was in the house with a killer. Deon loved Smitty like a little brother or an adoptive son and there was no way he would be suspicious of him in any way. Smitty's devotion to fight the war against the mob with Deon was odd because he had his whole life ahead of him, but he was willing to die in a war that made no sense. It also didn't make sense to Tony and Serena as they rushed back to the house.

While the mob was serious about getting rid of Deon, Smitty was already doing their dirty work for them because he had his own agenda. Smitty rubbed Serena the wrong way from the very first time they met. He was always too gung-ho for her. He was always trying to prove something and Serena could never figure out his angle. At first, she chalked it up to him being young and hot-headed, but Smitty's behavior was still questionable to her. Yet, she said nothing.

Blood Is Thicker Than Water

The biological connection to Wally Webster came about when Smitty's paternal grandmother reached out to his maternal grandmother in Boston. After the death of Wally, he supposedly left everything that he ever owned to his only son Wally "Smitty" Webster Jr. Smitty's father decided to call him by his middle name because he wanted his son to have his own identity, not just because of safety reasons, but also to keep him from being judged because of his father's illegal involvement. Since his dad was well-known in the underworld, he made every effort to keep his foes from finding out about his son. Wally Sr. wanted his son to have his own identity and a regular childhood, since he didn't have one. He didn't want his son to become a hustler like he did. He wanted more for his son and he tried his hardest to make that happen. However, karma is a bitch and it came back to bite Wally Sr. in the ass big time.

When Smitty's mother became pregnant with him, she lived in the Mission Hill housing project. It was there that his father met the young, pretty and sexy Darlene one day while she was coming home from Northeastern University. Darlene was so fine there was nothing that Wally wouldn't do to have her. She was in her junior year at the university when the two met. Times were a little hard for her in the projects, so she took advantage of the full academic scholarship offered by the university to the residents of the projects who matriculated well enough in high school to gain acceptance at the university. Darlene was a smart enough student at Madison High school to earn honor roll for four years straight at the high school. She also scored high enough on the SAT exam to earn a full scholarship at Northeastern University. However, the scholarship didn't provide any money for food or books. When Darlene met Wally, the baller, she was apprehensive about talking to him. His persistence paid off one day and he was finally able to get her schedule at school and he picked her up everyday from school. When the two first met, Darlene didn't have a phone at home. The welfare assistance her disabled mother received monthly was not enough for them to afford telephone service. Within a week, all that changed when Wally started supplying Darlene with enough money to buy everything from food, to clothes, furniture, books, phone service and even cable. Wally made life for Darlene so much easier, she had to fight to keep from falling for him.

Finally, Darlene realized falling for Wally wasn't a fight she was going to win, so she allowed her heart to direct her. The fact that Wally was a drug dealer was well-known to everyone in the projects. His reputation as a bad boy and ruthless killer preceded him, but Darlene never saw that side of him. She knew a sweet and tender Wally who didn't force her into anything. Wally even waited almost six months before he even tried to make-out with Darlene. And after discovering she was still a virgin, he waited another three months before the two finally slept together. Darlene was head over heels for Wally and he was impressed by her determination to get a college education and to leave the projects after graduation. Wally also had bragging rights as the first man to ever sleep with Darlene, and that alone placed Darlene at the top of his list of women. Wally had many women, but he loved none of them like he loved Darlene. He made her a priority and he never treated her with any disrespect. Still, that didn't keep him from sleeping around with a bunch of other women at the time.

It was after the fall semester of her senior year in college that Darlene found out she was pregnant with Wally's child. She was happy and sad at the same time.

Darlene wanted to embark on a career as an electrical engineer, but the pregnancy would halt her plans. After the pregnancy was revealed, Wally didn't want Darlene to stay in the projects any longer. He suggested she move to the suburbs to keep what he now called his family out of harm's way. However, Darlene declined because she would forfeit her academic scholarship if she left the projects. They finally agreed that she would move after graduation. Darlene finally graduated four months later and five months pregnant with little Wally in her stomach. Wally was excited about the prospect of having a son, but he wasn't ready to leave the streets alone. Instead, he decided to buy a house in the suburb of Hartford in Connecticut to keep his family away from the streets. Since Hartford was only an hour and a half drive from Boston, Wally didn't think it was a big deal.

At first, Darlene objected to the move, but when she finally laid eyes on the mansion that Wally had purchased and the brand new E-class, Mercedes Benz that came with the house, she was sold. Of course, Wally had many other reasons why he kept Darlene in Connecticut, but the main reason was to keep her away from his other women in Boston. As a hustler, Wally enjoyed pussy more than he enjoyed his money. He couldn't stay away from the ladies.

He also could always use his hustling as an excuse whenever he didn't want to go home to Darlene, and that's exactly what started happening. There would be other women finer than Darlene that came along and Wally would just neglect her for them. After a period of time, Darlene started getting frustrated with Wally. He wasn't as sweet and attentive to her anymore. He only came up on the weekend to pick up his son and to bring money for her. He wasn't even satisfying her sexually anymore, not that Wally was ever a great lover, but Darlene had no one to compare him to.

The lonelier Darlene grew, the hornier she became. When young Smitty started school, Darlene was at the house all by herself. Wally had made it clear to her that he didn't want her to work because he wanted her to focus on raising their son. She didn't even bother arguing with him about that, even though she had worked hard to earn her degree. She enjoyed being a homemaker, but there was no one there to share the home with. Her loneliness would change one day when she discovered the man delivering her mail everyday. He was tall, handsome, and brown-skinned with bedroom eyes. Wally wasn't what most women would refer to as handsome. He was more a provider. This handsome young man, who was closer in age with Darlene, was like Karl Malone, delivering the mail on time, every time and everyday. Darlene made herself available so he could get a glimpse of her beautiful frame everyday. The more he smiled, the more she started revealing herself to him. Darlene's sexy hazel eyes became a trap for the mailman. It finally got to the point where he couldn't help himself anymore. "I hope I'm not overstepping my boundaries, but I have to tell you that your house is the most beautiful house that I have ever delivered mail to," he said to her while smiling. "That's kind of you to say, but all the houses on the street are pretty much the same," she retorted. "Yeah, but none of them have a woman as beautiful as you living in them," he said while flirting with his eyes. He also took inventory of her succulent lips, perky breasts, nice and tight looking body before saying his goodbyes. "I'll see you tomorrow," she said in a little girl's crush voice.

The Affair

Not long after the mailman started flirting with Darlene, she started fantasizing about him. She would get moist every time she thought of him and she couldn't stop the flow. Darlene had even learned to masturbate because of the mailman. The flirtatious encounters only intensified her desire to allow the man into her house to have his way with her. About a week of innocent flirting came to a halt when Darlene decided to wear a little negligee when the mailman showed up to deliver the mail. Though his route required him to deliver the mail by a certain time, he couldn't resist being late an hour on this particular day. Darlene didn't know what came over her when she invited the mailman into the house that her baby's father had access to whenever he wanted. "Why don't you come in for a cup of coffee today?" she invited. "Sure," the mailman said without hesitation. Darlene had the coffeepot warming up about ten minutes before he showed up. It was just a matter of pouring the coffee into a cup for him. "You know I never got your name!" she yelled from the kitchen. "My name is Alonzo.

What's yours?" he asked before realizing his fumble. She arrived with two cups of coffee in hand, smiled and said, "I figured you knew my name, since you deliver my mail everyday." He seemed more nervous than usual, so she decided to cut him a little slack. "I understand. This is probably pretty unusual for you, huh? Not many of these white women in the area invite you in for coffee, right?" she said. "No ma'am," he said fumbling once more. "Ma'am? I don't think I'm that much older than you, but you can call me Darlene." "I'm sorry, Ma'am. I mean Darlene."

Alonzo was a little too nervous. After sharing a cup of coffee with Darlene, he left on his way to continue delivering the mail on his route. His shyness was even sexier to her. Since Wally was a take-charge, abrasive guy, she found Alonzo's demeanor refreshing. So, back she went to playing with herself in Alonzo's absence while thinking about him. As the two continued to conveniently run into each other, Alonzo finally developed enough nerve to one day pin Darlene on the couch for a voracious kiss. She had no idea it was coming, but she welcomed it when it did. Alonzo's lips were soft and sweet as she wrapped hers into his. She almost didn't want to let him go. They sat on the couch necking for almost twenty minutes before he left to finish his route.

That day, Alonzo left Darlene's house feeling like he had made strides to conquer the most beautiful woman he had ever seen. Darlene was drenched on the couch and her pussy was pulsating like it had never done before. She wanted Alonzo now more than ever. Since they restricted their necking to above the waist, she wondered if he was packing and what he could with his tool. He especially untucked his shirt to obstruct the bulge in his pants from her view.

Darlene had also become friends with one of her neighbors who happened to also be a housewife. She was part of a neighborhood watch committee they had formed, and the two of them blended right away. The two of them would talk endlessly on the phone while their kids were at school during the day. It was that neighbor who introduced Darlene to her first vibrator. Darlene had never experienced an orgasm with Wally while they were intimate. She had no idea what a climax was and when she finally discovered it, she was spending more money on double AA batteries than she did toilet paper. Darlene would use her vibrator four to five times a day to release stress. The more she came, the more she liked it. Sex with Wally was never the same as she became aware of his selfish ways in bed. He only cared about his own climax. The thought of Alonzo pouncing on her pussy made masturbation easier for her. She even named one of her vibrators after Alonzo.

Meanwhile, Alonzo no longer took his time delivering the mail. People in the neighborhood started getting their mail earlier than expected everyday, because Alonzo wanted to have extra time to spend with Darlene. A love affair was brewing and Darlene was becoming happier by the day. She and Alonzo would spend as much time as possible making out on the couch, without being found out by the neighbors. It was difficult for Darlene to reveal to Alonzo she had a man, but it was something that she had to do because Wally showed up at the house unannounced every time. His routine was mostly on the weekend to pick up Smitty, but whenever he was feeling horny during the week, he would come down to the house to break himself off a little something. Darlene had to make Alonzo aware of that. She explained to him that she had a son with Wally and he took care of her well, financially. At first, Alonzo didn't mind being the back door man, but as time progressed, he started to fall for Darlene, and she was also falling for him.

Make Love To Me

The necking, making-out and the masturbation to the image of Alonzo that Darlene had formed in her head had run its course. It was now time for the real thing. Darlene no longer wanted to pretend to be fucked. She wanted the real thing. The fact that they vacated their initial plan to keep their hands above the waist also didn't help. Though Alonzo seemed shy in the beginning, he was about to unleash his freak on Darlene. The fact that when she reached down to caress his crotch one day she felt a nine inch snake in his pants, only heightened her curiosity. She couldn't wait to get bitten by the big snake. Alonzo definitely was no rookie in the sack, and he proved that by demonstrating to Darlene his skills with only his fingers, leaving her to expect more than she ever had before from Wally.

The usual necking began after she closed the front door behind Alonzo. She looked around carefully before allowing him into her house. She wanted to make sure nobody on the block was keeping tabs on her. It really didn't matter because no one knew Wally, anyway. The black, flyaway apron, babydoll with matching thong, and black high heel shoes Darlene was wearing was enough to cause Alonzo to burst a blood vessel. He couldn't believe that this woman had birthed a child already. Her flat stomach, tiny waist and thick thighs were delectable as he stared at her standing before him. He had never had such a good view of Darlene before. Alonzo especially rushed his route that morning so he could have an extra hour to be with Darlene. "I hope you like what you see," she teased. His eyes lit up as she reached for his hand and brought him to the couch. "I see you're also happy to see me," she said as she reached for his crotch to feel his harden dick. She wouldn't get too far before Alonzo grabbed her from behind and pulled her towards him. He palmed her breasts in his hands and then ran them down her stomach as he left light trails of saliva on the back of her neck with his wet kisses. He blew on her neck to send chills down her body. "Mmmm," she murmured. He continued to run his hands down her stomach into her panties. He could feel her moisture. She was wet and ready to go.

Since time was on his side, Alonzo didn't want to rush things. He allowed his fingers to run wild over her clit as he continued to kiss her neck. The soft moans continued to escape her mouth each time his finger ran across her clit.

She even shook a little as she raised her arm to reach back around his neck. "You feel so good right now," she uttered. "You do too, baby. Are you ready for this?" he asked. "I've been ready for you for a while now. Make love to me," she told him. "I wanted to make love to you since the first time I laid eyes on you," he revealed. "Let's not wait another minute longer," she said as she turned around to kiss him. The kiss was long and passionate. It was as if time stood still while they explored each other's tongue. The soft pulling and tugging on each other's lips was magnified by Alonzo's hands caressing her perfect round ass, while she caressed his. Her 5ft 6inch frame and perfect size six body complimented his 6ft 1 inch, 180lbs frame perfectly. His perfectly toned physique only added to the allure of his sexiness. She yearned to be touched by such a man. Alonzo was doing all the right things.

With lips locked, the two slowly tiptoed to the back of the couch where Alonzo leaned her against it and started kissing her bare back. As his hands wandered forward around her body to unfasten her bra, his tongue took a tour down to her anus. The sensation of his tongue circling her anus sent a vibration throughout her body that forced her to tremble. "Oh my god! That shit is so good!" she exclaimed. Darlene never thought that a man could be so selfless with his loving. Alonzo almost made her climax with his tongue on her anus. He continued to lick down her thighs all the way to her ankles before he started making his way back up to her pussy. He turned her around with her legs spread apart and he took his tongue to her clit. She leaned on the back of the couch while placing one leg over his shoulder for better access to her pussy. "You taste so good, baby. I can eat your pussy all day," he confessed in between licks. Darlene held on to his bald head as her juice exited her body. "I'm coming! Don't stop! Oh yes!" she screamed while Alonzo ate her to ecstasy. This was the first time Darlene had ever climaxed with a man, and it was the sweetest thing she had ever experienced.

Alonzo was just getting started and Darlene was about to experience something she never thought was possible. Alonzo moved Darlene over to the seat of the couch for a little more sexual adventure. By now he had dropped his pants and underwear down to his ankles so he could commence the pussy whipping. Darlene finally got a full view of his huge dick. Though she had sucked Wally's dick in the past, it didn't look as delicious as Alonzo's. She reached for his dick while she sat on the couch and took it straight in her mouth. Alonzo automatically closed his eyes, expecting her to work her magic with her tongue.

Unfortunately, she lacked practice and her blowjob was a waste of time. Not one to crush a woman's ego, Alonzo allowed her to suck his dick only for a few minutes before he turned her around over the couch to commence his pussy assault. He already had a condom in hand, and by that time her legs were spread wide on her knees while holding the top part of the couch for support. Her ass was just beautiful and skin smooth like a baby's bottom. After rolling the extra large Lifestyle brand condom down his dick, Alonzo slowly penetrated Darlene. He filled her hole like a tire being plugged because of a leak. Her pussy was nice and tight. Alonzo started stroking her slowly as remnants of her pussy juice leaked out. The visual of his dick sliding in and out of her pussy was enough to make him succumb quicker than usual, but he held back and closed his eyes while holding on to her ass cheeks. The cadence of his strokes sent her into frenzy. "I have never had dick this good. Fuck me, baby!" she screamed out. "That pussy's good too," he retorted without missing a beat. Darlene pushed her ass back against his pelvis so she could get a deeper stroke. "That's my spot! That's it! Right there! Don't stop!" she begged. Alonzo stood still to allow her to get her nut. "Oh shit! I'm coming again!" she announced. Satisfied that she had climaxed again, it was time for Alonzo to go for his. He placed

Darlene on her stomach on the couch while her left leg hung near the floor. He had a tunnel view of her pussy from the back as he entered her pinkness. With his hands lightly smacking her ass cheeks, Alonzo started increasing the speed of his strokes. He could feel the nut trying to come out of his body and he was anxious. He stroked her hard and precise. 'Oh my fucking god you can fuck!" she assured him. He stroked her a few more times before he just collapsed on top of her while the condom caught all the white protein that left his body.

Alonzo and Darlene's affair became a regular thing. Though he couldn't take her out in public, he tried as much as he could to spend time with her at her house. He even wanted a relationship with her, but he knew she was a kept woman and his blue-collar job wasn't enough to entice her to leave her cushioned life.

What's The 411?

Wally had never developed trust for women for as long as he could remember. He was always busting one of his women cheating on him with another man, no matter how well he provided for her, as was the case with Darlene. It would've been fair for Wally to do a self-inventory to get to the root of his problem, but his ego wouldn't let him. In some weird way he thought his money more than made up for his lack of sexual prowess. In fact, he was too imposing for any woman to tell him he was not that good in bed. He just thought women were sluts and the only way to trust them was to spy on them.

Alonzo and Darlene never noticed the black, darkly tinted SUV parked about two blocks down the street from the house one day while he entered Darlene's house. They both thought the coast was clear, and as usual, their sexual romp lasted about an hour before Alonzo left to finish his route. Wally never really had any reason to be suspicious of Darlene in the past. She had never missed one of his phone calls. She always picked up the phone when it rang to assure

Wally she was home, but one day it was hard to pick up the phone while she had a dick in her mouth. Darlene was sucking the skin off Alonzo's dick when the phone rang repeatedly and she never ran to pick it up. She figured she'd tell Wally she went to run an errand. That probably would've worked if she had picked up the phone the second time he called, but it was even more difficult then because Alonzo had nine inches of blood flow penetrating Darlene's wall and climax was near. She needed to cum and the phone would have to wait. Darlene was starting to become addicted to Alonzo's dick. Wally wasted no time driving out to Hartford to check on Darlene. By then, Alonzo was long gone and she had washed every evidential sign of sex off her body.

Wally walked in the house angry and pissed. He wanted to walk in and kill somebody, but no one was there. "Where the fuck is he? Why didn't you answer the fucking phone?" he screamed at her. She didn't know what to say. She was silent for a second before his fist connected with her left eye, sending her flat on her back. She couldn't believe it, but she wasn't conscious enough to say anything. He pummeled her and threatened to kill her if she ever let the phone ring again, before he walked out of the house. She barely heard him, but when she came to, she knew she couldn't be with this man anymore, but leaving him would prove to be harder than she thought. Still, she was undeterred and Alonzo continued to sex her whenever she wanted it, but she started going to his house. The one time Alonzo decided to go in for a quickie, the Black SUV captured the whole thing on camera. That was enough for Wally to come back and deface her the same way he had defaced Serena years earlier. However, a custody battle would later ensue, and Wally lost because of the physical abuse he had inflicted upon her. He was ordered to pay her very little child support, because Wally didn't have a job or any of his businesses in his name. Everything was in his mother's name. Darlene's life changed after Wally reconstructed her face with his hands and feet. Alonzo was no longer interested in seeing her and Wally kicked her out of the house.

Because Darlene had never worked since she graduated from college, she had a hard time getting a job. The fifty-dollars-a-week child-support she was getting from Wally could barely sustain her financially. She ended up moving into a housing project in Hartford called, Stowe Village. It was there that Darlene started meeting all the bad people in her life that she shouldn't have met. Her life spiraled out of control and she fell victim to heroin. She started using drugs daily to cope with life, but she never could control her drug use. Her son also noticed how his mother was struggling, so he decided to become a drug dealer to help feed the family. Darlene ended up dying sooner rather than later, leaving her young son to fend for himself in a cruel place.

In the meantime, Wally's mother had established a special trust fund for her grandson with all the money she received from Wally. Smitty was left with his grandmother every weekend when Wally brought him to Boston during the first couple of years when he was able to see his son. After Wally went to court and didn't win custody of his son, he pretty much turned his back on mother and child. However, as a grandmother, Ms. Webster was always kind and loving to her only grandson. She knew her son's dealings were illegal, but she wanted to make sure he didn't leave her grandson without anything in case he became a statistic of the game. Wally was like a saint to his mother. She had never seen his demonic side. He blamed Darlene for keeping his son from him. He never told his mother the real story about the physical pain he inflicted on his son's mother. Darlene also never mentioned to her son that his dad had beaten her to a pulp and disfigured her to the point where she lost her beauty and became unrecognizable to the people who loved her.

Ms. Webster continued to make deposits into the account for Smitty until the death of his father. She searched for him and never could find him, but after Wally was killed by the Hoodfellas, Ms. Webster drove to Hartford and was able to get information on her grandson. His maternal grandmother gave Darlene's address in Hartford to his paternal grandmother. When she finally did get a hold of Smitty, she told him who his father was and how his father loved him, but more importantly, she made him believe that his father had left behind the five million dollars he now had in a trust fund. Ms. Webster glorified her son while enraging her grandson, Smitty, when she talked about how the Hoodfellas were jealous of his dad's success and how they plotted to kill him and take all his money. She didn't really know the real story, but bits and pieces of rumors she heard in the hood allowed her to concoct an angry enough story to tell Smitty and convinced him to exact revenge on his father's killers.

Smitty's Plan

Smitty was angry and on killer mode after his grandmother told him the story. Revenge was the only thing he had on his mind. He thought about all those times that he had to eat mayonnaise sandwiches with sugar water in the projects, and how shamefully his mother died. His grandmother fueled him with anger as she made his father look like a man that any little boy would proudly call daddy. Smitty wanted to get next to Deon any way he could. An opportunity came knocking when he joined a crew of killers in Boston that the Hoodfellas decided to hire. He figured he could take that opportunity to show his heart on the streets and his loyalty to the Hoodfellas, by showing Deon he was a killer. The opportunity to join the Hoodfellas in Haiti was perfect for Smitty. He wanted to go to Haiti, kill the whole crew and come back to the States knowing he had avenged his father's death and would return back to the States without having to look over his shoulders for the rest of his life. However, things didn't go as smoothly as he expected in Haiti. All the roadblocks the Hoodfellas faced with

Deon's kidnapping took away his focus and he had to act like a soldier. During the shootout with Antoine's crew and Reginald's crew, Smitty unsuccessfully tried to take Deon out. Every time he aimed his gun near Deon, another member of the Hoodfellas was nearby and he had to change course. Though he seemed like a hothead and wanted the Hoodfellas to think he was crazy, Smitty was very calculated. He wanted to engage the Hoodfellas in battle with the Haitian Posse so he could have the opportunity to take out Deon. There are always casualties in the midst of war and Smitty wanted to make sure that Deon became a casualty for killing his dad.

The day of reckoning started when the mob decided to strong-arm their way into the Luxurious Life, LLC. That situation gave Smitty the opening that he had been waiting for all this time. Unfortunately, Mike was the first casualty of Smitty's deadly vengeance. Mike was the perfect target because he and Smitty had developed an open bond. They even went out to a strip club the night before his death to celebrate. Smitty wanted to send him off the best way possible, so he rented a room and called on the two girls, Chocolate and Honey whom he took back to the hotel with him from Mean T's party, to come by to entertain Mike. It was the first time Mike ever had a threesome with two women. He was the happiest, but that happiness wouldn't last for long. After the ladies left, they called Smitty to pick up Mike from the hotel. Instead of driving Mike home as planned, Smitty made a detour and took him to a field where he shot him once in the back of the head. After confirming Mike was dead, he then took out a knife and cut across Mike's body to implicate the mob. Afterwards, he dropped the body off in front the Luxurious Life, LLC office. At that point his plan was working and everybody in the Hoodfellas camp thought the mob was responsible for Mike's death.

Since the mob came in to make a demand for money a few days later, Deon automatically associated the mob with Mike's killing. Smitty's plan worked perfectly. He created a war between the mob and the Hoodfellas. The mob didn't actually retaliate against them until the death of Giuseppe. The mob boss ordered a hit on Deon after Giuseppe was killed, but they wanted to carry the hit out in public. They wanted to send a clear message to all the members of the Hoodfellas that if anybody wanted to stand with Deon, they were going to be killed.

Smitty continued with his plan and decided to kill Evelyne in the parking lot to infuriate Deon. If Deon hadn't lost his cool, he would've figured out Evelyne was shot by somebody inside the car. Smitty was a born killer. He didn't give a damn about anybody's life. However, his motive also changed when Deon decided to put his name as a beneficiary on his estate in case something happened to him. Deon had started treating Smitty more like a son than a little brother. He wanted to make sure the kid was going to be alright. He had bought out Tweak's mom and owned one hundred percent of the business, even though he kept her name on the papers to avoid legal issues. He had a personal conversation with Smitty and told him that his plan was to have Smitty take over the business. In addition, Deon also told Smitty about fifty-million dollars he had stashed in the house in case of an emergency. Smitty was filled with hate, envy and greed, but continued to use the death of his father as motivation to go after Deon. He stood to gain everything that his father ever lost if he killed Deon.

Smitty also understood that Crusher was Deon's right hand man and he had to get rid of him in order to gain full access to Deon. The murderous rampage also started to become fun to Smitty. He would laugh inside every time the Hoodfellas thought the mob was attacking them and killing off their personnel one by one. Deon was no ballistic expert, but if he had checked the bullets on the door panel of the Range Rover, he would've known that all the bullets came from Crusher's guns. Crusher didn't anticipate the cold barrel of Smitty's gun against his temple about three miles down the street from the house. "You have reached your destination, player," Smitty told Crusher after pulling out his gun and stuck it to his face. "Yo, what the fuck are you doing?" Crusher asked. "Don't worry about it," Smitty told him as he pulled the trigger twice. Crusher's slumped body lay dead in the passenger seat. Smitty went around the car and unloaded Crusher's weapon against the car. The bullet-riddled truck looked like it just came out of Iraq, but Smitty managed to make Deon believe he miraculously escaped without a scratch on him.

Tony started to become suspicious of the events, but he said nothing because Smitty seemed like a trustworthy guy to Deon. Tony hadn't been around long enough to meddle in Deon's business, so he let it roll off his back. He did notice that it was the second time that two of Deon's crewmembers died the same way. Smitty had no idea that Tony's suspicion rose after the death of Crusher. He had demonstrated his heart and loyalty to Deon in Haiti, so he felt confident that he would be able to get away with his covert operation.

Smitty didn't care too much for Serena because she had taken on the role of the matriarch of the family. She knew her son was in charge, but she wanted everyone to know that she was special, and she wouldn't allow anybody to disrespect her. Smitty thought about killing her just for the hell out of it one day, because of an incident that took place in the kitchen. Smitty was too lazy to pour himself a glass of orange juice, so he decided to take the carton to the head and then put the carton of juice back in the fridge. He never saw Serena standing there watching him. "I know you ain't gonna put your mouth on that and then turn around and put it back in the fridge, right?" Serena asked sarcastically. Smitty was startled, but said nothing back to Serena. He was thinking to himself, *I can't wait to kill her ass.* That was the first time Serena noticed Smitty's trifling ways. She kept her eyes on him and he kept her eyes on her, all the while acting like everything was cool. He gave her an off the cuff apology for what he had done, but he was truly resentful that he had been caught. He was walking around the house with a lot of hate in his heart.

Smitty was proud that he was able to convince Deon that Crusher had been shot by the mob. The delirium going on was amusing to him. He knew Deon was losing it and it was a matter of time before the people around him bailed on him. When Tony and Serena decided to leave, Smitty was glad because it was two less people that he had to kill. He did plan on wiping out everybody. For the first time since he joined the Hoodfellas, he saw weakness in Deon. The confusion that the killings had caused forced Deon to expose his vulnerable side. Smitty was laughing inside. He couldn't wait to have his moment of glory.

Smitty's final plan was to kill Deon and Cindy after Tony and Serena left, but he didn't do it because he needed the combination to the safe to get the rest of the money from the house. Though Deon had told Smitty about the stash in the safe, he had never revealed the combination. It wasn't until he was leaving for Boston for his meeting with Tommy Li that he revealed to Smitty and Cindy the combination of the safe in case he needed them to take a private plane to bring the money to Boston to pay the Chinese Connection, if they had agreed to assist them with the mob. Smitty actually caught a lucky break, because he had planned to torture Deon and Cindy until the combination for the safe was revealed.

After dropping Deon off at the airport, Smitty contemplated killing Cindy right away after he got in the house, but he didn't kill her because when they got back to the house, she started reminiscing about the time she met Deon in Boston. She ended up telling Smitty the whole story of how Deon took out Wally at the Webster mansion, which fueled Smitty's desire to torture and kill both of them. Cindy painted a heroic picture of Deon against Wally, and Smitty hated every minute of it. He wanted Deon to know that he wasn't afraid of him and he was going to kill everyone he loved.

Smitty's grandmother made him feel like his father was the best man that ever lived. She wanted him to admire the idea of the man he never knew. She talked about the admiration that everyone had for his father and how an envious Deon plotted to take over his fortune. Smitty wanted to relive the dream. He had the heart of a hustler and the thirst of a killer, which made for a deadly combination. However, Smitty should've tried to learn the real story with his dad from somebody who really knew it.

The Real Story

Wally Webster Sr. had always been a good son to his mother. He moved her out of the projects and gave her a life of luxury when he started attaining success. There was no limit to what he would do for his mom. Ms. Webster struggled with young Wally when he was a kid. His dad was shot by another man during a dispute over a crap game. Ms. Webster relied on government assistance to survive. Until the age of twelve, Wally had never eaten anything but generic brand food. The food stamps his mom collected were only good enough to buy the generic brand items at the supermarket. The kids at Wally's school often made fun of his clothes and shoes, and as a result, he started getting into a lot of fights. By the age of twelve, Wally was ready to help bring home the bacon. He started hustling for an older drug dealer in the projects who showed him the ropes in the game. By the time Wally was fourteen years old, he was earning more money than the teachers at his school. They had a hard time keeping his attention in class. Wally was not interested in what they had to teach him. He was all about making money. He was often picked up on truancy warrants for missing school, but they could never keep him. By age sixteen, Wally decided to completely forgo school to start building his empire on the street. As he climbed the street pharmaceutical ladder, he started spoiling his mother by spending lots of money on her. He vowed that she would never have to work and he would make more money than a superstar athlete to take care of her. Wally delivered on his promise when he became the biggest hustler in Boston, earning millions of dollars when he was just nineteen years old.

Unfortunately, Wally picked up a bad habit from his father, which was domestic violence. He didn't know how to control his temper and reacted violently against women. Growing up in a household where his dad forced his mom to submit with his fist, influenced Wally greatly. The situation with Serena was only the tip of the iceberg when Wally got violent to the point where he disfigured a woman. This behavior would continue and eventually Darlene, Smitty's mom, would suffer the same fate. However, Wally didn't stop there. After learning from the court that he couldn't have custody of his son, Smitty, Wally decided to turn Darlene into a drug addict. He introduced her to heroin and got her addicted to the drug so the court would give him custody of Smitty. Ms. Webster never saw that side of her son. She only knew the loving side and that was the story she told her grandson to enrage him, so that he could look up to his father in good memory. She never anticipated she would be creating a monster with her stories.

Smitty didn't have any memory of his father lashing out at his mom because he was always out of the house when it happened. At least Wally was smart enough not to expose his son to the violence that he grew up witnessing from his own father. Even when Darlene started getting high, Wally always made sure his son was out of the house, so he couldn't see it. Wally had decided to turn his back on Smitty after losing so many battles in the court system. It was Ms. Webster who was relentless about keeping in touch with her grandson. In a way, she wanted to give Smitty what she could've never given to her own son. Ultimately, her desire to keep her son's name in good standing with her grandson ended up costing Smitty his life.

The Mob

Meanwhile, the mob's relentless pursuit of Deon's head continued. They had been staking out Deon's house for weeks and wanted to wipe out the crew at once. The mob decided to make their move the day Smitty picked up Deon from the airport. The arrival of Serena and Tony to the house was also noticeable as the cab dropped them off in front of the house. The mob figured the whole family was together and it was time to wipe them out. The daytime security guard at the gate only felt the butt of the .38 special hitting the back of his head before his lights went out. He had no recollection of the incident. He woke up to find himself bound, gagged and naked in the small security booth. One of the Italian mobsters took off the security guard's uniform so he could wear it and act like he was security for the complex. The other residents driving in and out of the gated community never noticed anything unusual. The security at the gate greeted them as normal and none of them cared to ask if he was a new hire. Each house in the gated community sat on five sprawling acres of land near the ocean. Each home also had its own private gate and six foot wall for additional privacy. The mob knew exactly where their target was located and they had better move fast to get the job done right.

Serena and Tony didn't have much time on their hands as Deon bled profusely from the four gunshot wounds he suffered at the hand of Smitty, on his thigh, shoulder leg and arm. Thankfully none of his wounds were fatal. As Tony sprung Deon over his shoulder to get him in the car, Serena held the door to the garage open so they could get in. The closest hospital was less than five miles away, so there was no reason to panic yet. As Serena backed the Benz out of the driveway, she was met with a hail of bullets coming from a group of white men who exited two black vans with machine guns in their hands. She quickly put the car back in drive and pulled back into the garage. Life itself was slipping from their hands as the mob continued to unload clip after clip of bullets their way. While running and dodging for cover in between the cars in the garage, Serena pulled out her own weapon so she could fire back at the mob. Tony quickly pressed the automatic button to closed the garage door. "I have two guns in the glove compartment," Deon managed to murmur to Tony. "We need to get him in the house. I'll cover you while you get him out," Serena suggested. Deon was a pretty big guy and there was no way Serena could carry him out of the backseat of the car into the house. She moved towards the gate of the garage and broke one of the glasses while shielding herself behind the frame in the corner. Serena started to return fire with her automatic weapons. One of the mob guys went down with a bullet to the chest. As the fire exchange continued, the mob assassins retreated behind the vans for cover. Serena didn't stop shooting until she ran out of bullets and Tony was inside the house.

The three of them were trapped in the house as the mobsters continued to shoot, while pouring gasoline around the mansion. Serena, Tony and Deon were crawling on their stomachs the whole time to keep from getting shot. Though Deon was ready to die, he did not want to die like that. Within seconds, the house was engulfed in flames and the mob stood there to make sure no one exited the house. Neighbors called the cops when they heard gunshots, but the cops didn't respond until the house was burned to a crisp and the mob was long gone. The mob had accomplished their mission. They assassinated Deon and his family in their own home. They had won the war and the Hoodfellas were no longer.

The mob boss smiled from ear to ear when it was reported on the news that five unidentified dead bodies had been found at the house. The cops claimed there were multiple gas explosions at the house, which set off what sounded like a chain reaction of gunshots, as initially reported by the neighbors. To keep the neighbors in the ritzy neighborhood from panicking, the cops concocted that story for the mob. To put it simple and plain, a gas line started leaking and it set off an explosion that killed everybody in the house, according to the police investigation.

Exit Wounds

Living in the back woods of South Carolina was not the life that Deon had ever imagined for himself. Serena, Tony and Deon barely escaped the house alive when it went up in flames. As they crawled around on the floor to the secret passage of the house that Deon had especially built under the house after he purchased it where he also kept his safe, they almost got caught in the fire. Tony was fast on his feet as he opened the safe to clear out the last fifty million dollars that Deon had to his name. The three of them crawled on their stomachs towards the water to make it to the canoe that Deon kept below the dock behind his home. While the mob was busy watching the house go up in flames, they never believed that Deon and his crew could escape the massive fire. After the three of them got in the canoe, Tony pretty much weaved his way in and out between the big yachts docked on the water. Tony had to use all his strength to row the boat to the other end of the dock so they could get away. A rich couple became the victim of their getaway when they left the engine on their speedboat running while they put on their life vests on the dock. Tony quickly jumped on the boat and untied the rope that kept it from floating back to sea. He then pulled Deon and Serena on board as they took off towards the Keys.

They never made it to the hospital with Deon. They got lucky when a money-hungry doctor with a taste for luxury decided he couldn't pass up a few million dollars to stitch Deon's wounds. Serena pleaded with him to save her son. The doctor was recognized when he exited his LS model Lexus to go to his docked boat. The identifying license plate with the big MD in front of the numbers was enough for Serena to identify the man as a doctor. No one even noticed the three of them as Serena and Tony climbed up on the dock pulling Deon's bloodied body up, hoping to catch a cab to the hospital to get him help. The doctor was nonchalantly making his way to the boat when Serena approached him for help. He had no reservation about helping until he saw the gunshot wounds on a bloody Deon. He hesitated at first. However, his refusal to help was denied when Tony pulled out a 9mm and stuck it to his head. "Look Doc, I ain't trying to kill you or nothing, but you're gonna save my son's life today. We're good people, but don't turn this to a bad situation," Tony warned. The doctor was shaking as they descended in his yacht so he could start working on Deon.

As the doctor worked on Deon on his boat, Serena stood guard to make sure no one was paying attention to them. Deon and Tony's clothes were covered in blood. The doctor worked his miracle and he assured them that Deon would be okay. However, Tony didn't trust that the doctor would just let them get away so easily. He offered the doctor five million dollars if he never reported them to the police, but he also needed the doctor's car in order to make it out of Florida. "Look Doc, this situation don't have anything to do with you and it won't affect you in any way. We have been victimized here and we're just trying to get outta town. We appreciate your help and we're willing to pay you for your time and your silence. We don't want to hurt you, but please don't force our hands," Tony warned him again. The doctor couldn't believe his eyes when he saw the five million dollars in cash offered to him. "Here, take the car," he said as he tossed his keys to Tony. He even offered Tony and Deon a change of clothes in case they got pulled over by the cops. The blood-soaked shirts and pants they were wearing would have made them an easy target for the cops in case they got pulled over. The doctor's life was about to change forever with this much money. In the process, he forgot to take his house keys off the key chain. "I think you might need these to start your boat and to get into your house, doc," Tony said to him as he tossed him back the rest of the keys. Tony promised to have the doctor's car shipped back to him within a couple of days as the three of them got on the road to South Carolina. The fact that the plate on the doctor's car announced to the world he was a medical doctor worked perfectly for Tony as he drove up to South Carolina from Florida. The cops didn't even bother him, not even once. After all, they don't usually bother doctors behind the wheel.

As planned, the doctor's car was delivered back to the dock where it was taken. He never reported the incident to the police, but he upgraded his boat and lifestyle a few months later. Deon, Serena and Tony have been living peacefully in the back woods of South Carolina where they purchased a two-thousand-acre farm with two sprawling homes from a white man who did time with Tony for killing his wife after catching her in bed with another man. The cash transaction stayed between them, as the man quietly transferred the property into Deon's name.

The fact that Deon had the three decatpitated heads delivered to his home, turned out to work in his favor. The five human skulls found at his mansion in Florida after the fire was put out, belonged to Smitty, Case and his two boys and Cindy. The mob believed they were all the people in the house and the Hoodfellas family in its entirety was killed. It took Deon some time to recover from his wounds, but he was back on his feet again and hoping to live life in obscurity and to have a family with some children of his own some day.

Unfortunately, Deon never made it to Crusher's funeral. He had Crusher's body shipped to Boston to his family and he later sent a check to Crusher's mother from his share of the Hoodfellas.

A Changed Life

The members of the mosque were enamored by the young minister who made the Quran an easy lifestyle to adhere to. While most ministers treat the Bible or the Quran like a book, Minister Deon X made it his lifestyle. He lived by the word and believed in the word. After moving to South Carolina, Tony decided it was best for him to return to his religious roots of Islam to live a better, happy and prosperous life. After marrying Serena in a private ceremony, she also followed in her husband's footsteps and converted to Islam. However, Tony was happiest when Deon decided to devote his life to Islam as well. After realizing that the street life was long behind him and the Hoodfellas were long gone, Deon started to figure out his purpose in the next phase of his life. One day after driving over two hours to North Charleston, South Carolina from their home to attend a service at a temple with Abdul Mustafa Muhammad, his stepfather's now legal name and mother, Serena Muhammad, Deon was convinced that Islam was his calling. Seeing his life flashed before him when he was shot, after recovering from his wounds, Deon's fervor for life took on a new course. He studied the Quran ferociously. He started reading about his new idols, Malcolm X, Minister Louis Farrakhan and The Honorable Elijah Muhammad. Deon was impressed with the work of the Muslims in the black community and he wanted to become an extension of that work.

Deon made the two-hour drive with his mother and Abdul every week to the temple. He dedicated his life to Islam, and he wanted to help the Muslim brothers released from prison with nowhere and no one to go to when they came home. Deon decided to turn part of his two-thousand-acre farm to use so he could help provide work for the brothers who would most likely be shunned by society because of their incarceration. As the brothers came home by the droves, Deon decided to build a new community for Muslims where people least expected it, in the boondocks of South Carolina. Homes were built to accommodate the growing population moving to his newfound community, and jobs were established to keep the community self-sufficient and sustainable. Deon's new company of natural food products reached sales of twenty million dollars in the first year of business. The community thrived beyond expectation and every newly released inmate had a new lease on life.

Minister Louis Farrakhan visited the new community and gave it his stamp of approval. It was with his blessings that Deon X became a minister and built a new temple in South Carolina so the brothers, sisters and the children of the new Muslim community could practice their faith without having to drive almost two hours every week to North Charleston, South Carolina. "All praises due to Allah," Deon told the brothers and sisters at the temple after delivering a fiery message that morning. Everyone was on their feet as they applauded the young minister. His new wife and two sons were also proud of him, but more importantly, Abdul and Serena couldn't ask for a better son.

The End

Sample Chapters

From the book series

KWAME

By
Richard Jeanty

Chapter I

The Hero

The two men standing guard at the door didn't even see him coming. The loud thump of a punch to the throat of the six-foot-five-inch giant guarding the door with his life had the breath taken right out of him with that one punch. He stumbled to the ground without any hope of ever getting back up. His partner noticed the swift and effective delivery of the man's punch, and thought twice about approaching him. Running would be the smartest option at this time, but how cowardice would he look? The attacker was but five feet ten inches tall and perhaps one hundred and ninety pounds in weight. The security guard didn't have time on his side and before he could contemplate his next move, the attacker unloaded a kick to his groin that sent his six foot seven inch frame bowing in pain while holding his nuts for soothing comfort. Another blow to the temple followed and the man was out permanently.

At first glance, Kwame didn't stand a chance against the two giants guarding the front door. One weighed just a little less than three hundred and twenty five pounds, and the other looked like an NFL lineman at three hundred and sixty pounds. However, Kwame was a trained Navy Seal. He came home to find that the people closest to him were embroiled in a battle that threatened their livelihood daily. His sister, Candice, became a crackhead while his mother Aretha was a heroin addict. Two different types of drugs in one household, under one roof was enough to drive him crazy. Kwame didn't even recognize his sister at first. She had aged at least twice her real age and his mother was completely unrecognizable. He left her a strong woman when he joined the Navy eight years prior, but he came back to find his whole family had been under the control of drug dealers and the influence of drugs and Kwame set out to do something about it.

The two giants at the door was just the beginning of his battle to get to the low level dealers who controlled the streets where he grew up. As he made his way down the long dark corridor, he could see women with their breasts bare and fully naked, bagging the supplies of drugs for distribution throughout the community. Swift on his feet like a fast moving kitten, he was unnoticeable. He could hear the loud voices of men talking about their plans to rack up another half a million dollars from the neighborhood through their drug distribution by week's end. The strong smell of weed clouded the air as he approached the doorway to meet his nemesis. Without saying a word after setting foot in the room, he shot the first man who took noticed of him right in the head. Outnumbered six to one and magazine clips sitting on the tables by the dozen and loaded weapons at reach to every person in the room, Kwame had to act fast. It was a brief stand off before the first guy reached for his Nine Millimeter automatic weapon, and just like that he found himself engulfed in a battle with flying bullets from his chest all the way down to his toes. Pandemonium broke and everybody reached for their guns at once. As Kwame rolled around on his back on the floor with a Forty Four Magnum in each hand, all five men were shot once in the head and each fell dead to the floor before they had a chance to discharge their weapons.

The naked women ran for their lives as the barrage of gunshots sent them into frenzy. The masked gun man dressed in all black was irrelevant to them. It was time to get the hell out of dodge, to a safe place away from the crackhouse. Not worried too much about the innocent women, Kwame pulled out a laundry bag and started filling it with the stack of money on the table. By the time he was done, he had estimated at least a million dollars was confiscated for the good of the community. The back door was the quickest and safest exit without being noticed. After throwing the bag of money over a wall separating the crack house from the house next door, Kwame lit his match and threw it on the gasoline that he had poured before entering the house. The house was set ablaze and no evidence was left behind for the cops to build a case. It was one of the worse fires that Brownsville had seen in many years. No traces of human bones were left, as everything burned town to ashes by the time the New York Fire Department responded.

Kwame had been watching the house for weeks and he intended on getting rid of everything including the people behind the big drug operation that was destroying his community. Before going to the front of the house to get rid of the security guards, he had laid out his plan to burn down the house if he couldn't get passed them. A gallon of gasoline was poured in front of all the doors except the front one where the two securities stood guard. His plan was to start the fire in the back and quickly rush to the front to pour out more gasoline to block every possible exit way, but that was his last option. His first option was to grab some of the money to begin his plans for a recreational center for the neighborhood kids. His first option worked and it was on to the next crew.

When Kwame came home he vowed to work alone to get rid of the bad elements in his neighborhood. Mad that he had to leave home to escape the belly of the beast, Kwame came back with a vengeance. He wanted to give every little boy and little girl in his neighborhood a chance at survival and a future. He understood that the military did him some good, but he had to work twice as hard to even get considered for the elite Navy Seals. The military was something that he definitely didn't want any boys from his neighborhood to join. For him it was a last resort and in the end he made the best of it. Guerilla warfare was the most precious lesson he learned while in the military and it was those tactics that he planned on using to clean up his neighborhood.

A one man show meant that only he could be the cause to his own demise. There'd be no snitches to worry about, no outside help, no betrayal and most of all no deception from anybody. Self reliance was one of the training tactics he learned in the Navy and it was time for him to apply all that he learned to make his community all it could be.

Getting rid of that crack house was one of the first priorities of his mission. Kwame knew that the crack houses were sprouting all over the neighborhood and it would take precise planning on his part to get rid of them in a timely fashion without getting caught by the police. Kwame also knew that he wasn't just going to be fighting the drug dealers, but some of the crooked cops that are part of the criminal enterprise plaguing the hood.

Sample chapter from Mr. Erotica
By

Richard Jeanty

The Sexual Exploits at My Wedding

According to Kevin, "Big jugs Becky," as he called her, was not wearing any panties when she lured him into the women's bathroom for a quickie. She flashed one of her big breasts to Kevin as he was walking to the men's room with a Heineken in his hand and trying not to pee on himself. She then followed with her index finger motioning for him to come towards her. She had been paying attention to Kevin all night as he put his dance moves on some of the female guests on the dance floor. The fact that Kevin managed at least a six pack of Heineken within an hour at the reception, helped to loosen him up with the ladies. Becky's imagination must've gone wild as she saw the gyrating waist of Kevin caressing the hips of the sisters to the rhythm of the Hip Hop beat. Kevin was the best dancer of all of us. Not only was he a bad boy, he also danced like one. Many of the women at the party already knew who he was because of the success of his first street novel, The Game is Mine, which I published under my publishing company, Stories R Us.

Feeling like a celebrity, Kevin was dancing the night away and lining up women for later that night in the process. Though his book was primarily about "Street life," Kevin's edgier sex chronicles found their way to the pages of his book and the women were more than eager to learn if his imagination really pushed the sexual limits in real life. There was one scene about a man fucking this woman in the middle of a hallway, and that scene kept the female readers asking for more. And even his male readers had to give him props on a job well done. Becky's silicone-filled titties were hard as a rock, but they looked perky to Kevin as her nipples protruded through the silk dress she was wearing. "You got some moves there, handsome," she said to Kevin. "Oh yeah? How about you show me some of your moves?" Kevin said as he backed her up into the bathroom. He stood directly behind the bathroom door to keep any intruder from entering, while he dropped his pants to his ankles and his ten-inch dick was sticking up, ready to invade Becky's pussy. But first, Kevin realized he hadn't peed yet and he really needed to before he got started with Becky. Kevin, a little inebriated, found himself peeing on everything except the toilet. "Are you ok in there?" Becky asked as she heard the full strength of Kevin's piss hitting the bathroom wall and the floor. The women's bathroom was a complete mess by the time Kevin was done.

Still undeterred by the mess Kevin made in the stall, Becky was ready to take his dick in her mouth as he repositioned himself by the door. "Let's move over near the sink," she suggested, so they could have more room and comfort. "Nah, I want to stand by the door so no one can get in," he said to her. "I already locked the door, silly," she confirmed. Kevin started laughing because he hadn't noticed the lock on the door. "Well, let's do this then," he said as he grabbed his dick and directed her mouth to it. Becky happily squatted down, holding her dress up to keep it from hitting the floor, while the other held Kevin's dick as she wrapped her lips on the shaft of it to experience his ten inches of pleasure. "Your cock is beautiful and big," she said between licks. Kevin's face was gleeful as Becky's thin lips and smooth tongue went up and down and around his dick. The blowjob would go on for about five minutes until Kevin pulled her up to him to suck on her fake titties. Realizing that her titties looked better than they tasted, Kevin moved on to her wet pink pussy, filling every inch of it with his fingers after lifting up her long dress. He soon bent her over the sink, lifted her dress and penetrated her from behind. Never one to leave his house without a condom, Kevin wrapped himself in a Lifestyle extra sensitive before he commenced the pussy assault.

With a hand full of bleached blond hair, Kevin pounded Becky's pussy from behind. "Fuck me with that big black cock," she kept whispering like a porn star. "You love this black dick, huh?" Kevin asked as he fucked her with rage. "Yes! Fuck me! I love your cock!" she screamed in a low tone. Kevin wrapped his hand around her neck as he tried to split open her pussy with his big dick. The more forceful he got with her, the more excited she became and the more she wanted him to fuck her. "Oh my gosh! This is what I call fucking!" Becky exclaimed. Kevin was laughing inside because he knew that he was fucking this white woman the way that a former slave would exact revenge on a plantation owner's daughter.

Kevin turned Becky around and sat her on the sink. He brought her ass to the edge of the sink as he inserted his entire dick inside her. Becky couldn't keep her eyes closed as she moaned in ecstasy. A few minutes later she was holding on for dear life as Kevin made her cum like she never came before on the bathroom sink. Becky didn't want Kevin to leave unsatisfied. "I want you to fuck me in the ass," she suggested. The suggestion alone had Kevin damn near busting a nut before he even penetrated her. Kevin had never had anal sex before. It was new and exciting territory to him. Becky's asshole wasn't as tight as he imagined, but he was still excited none the less. Watching his dick move in and out of Becky's ass with ease was a thrill and he soon shouted, "I'm coming!" She turned around, pulled his condom off, and took his dick down her throat to suck every drop of semen from his dick.

Becky and Kevin never saw the two female spectators standing by the last stall in the bathroom. "I'm next!" one of them yelled. "No, I'm next!" the other one exclaimed. "Ladies, there's enough of me to go around. How about a threesome in my room later on?" he suggested as he handed them a spare key to his room with the room number on the card. The two obviously good friends, agreed to meet Kevin in his room after the reception.

Rammell's account of his sexual tryst was no less exciting. According to him, the young slim and petite brunette started smiling at him while he was lounging in the lobby after coming off a long stint on the dance floor with her. He wasn't thinking that it was nothing more than a dance, but she enjoyed his moves so much, she followed him to the lobby for more conversation. "Are you from Boston?" she asked with a tempted grin. "Yes, I'm from Mattapan," Rammell told her. No names were exchanged, but they somehow found themselves stuck in the elevator on the tenth floor and the brunette was servicing Rammell like he had never been serviced before. It started with a flirtatious comment about Rammell's bulging crouch while they were dancing. "Were you happy to be dancing with me or did you have a roll of quarters in your pocket?" she asked playfully. "A pack of quarters are far smaller than what you felt, and I was a lot harder than that," he retorted. "How about you show me how hard you are and what kind of roll you're packing?" she assertively told him. "The pleasure would be all mine," Rammell told her.

After searching around for any sign of a camera, Rammell and the brunette started making out in the elevator as they made their way up. By the time they reached the tenth floor, the urge to pull the "emergency stop" button couldn't be contained. The brunette grabbed a hold of Rammell's nine-inch dick and took it in her mouth with a big smile. She slobbed on it until it could get no harder. They knew that management would soon come to their rescue as the alarm continued to go off, so Rammell tried to rush a quick nut before the doors could be opened. He started humping her mouth very quickly until semen started oozing out of his dick and into the back of her throat, as he was holding on to her head. "Oh shit! I'm coming!" Rammell hissed as the white, thick substance exited his penis. "I want it all down my throat," the brunette said while squeezing it all out of Rammell's dick.

Before maintenance could force open the elevator door, Rammell had released the emergency button and the brunette had wiped her mouth clean with a napkin. Both got off of the elevator to walk back to the reception with Rammell feeling a little light on his feet and more jovial than usual.

Their sexual trysts remind me of the fun that I had with Marsha's friends when I was a gigolo. I could only smile when my boys told me their little stories. If only they knew what I had been doing a few months prior to my wedding day. They would go nuts with envy.

Sample chapter from Cater To Her
By

Sean Mitchell

"Promiscuous Girl"

Angelica

"Doesn't your job require that you try out the merchandise before you buy it?" My best friend Rochelle laughed as we enjoyed early morning gossip over caramel frappuccino and blueberry biscotti in the food court of Garden State Plaza.

"I don't even know what his tongue tastes like." I laughed while looking down at my beautiful canary yellow diamond engagement ring.

"You got to be joking?" Rochelle paused for effect and then put her face into her hand as soon as I shook my head no.

Rochelle John was what I call a brick house. I know people use the term loosely. Some people get big-boned or just plain ole fat confused with being a brick house. For example, the comedian Monique ain't a brick house, maybe after a couple of hours on the treadmill for an entire year straight she could possibly become one. Beyonce's a brick house, nice wide set hips and an ass that won't make men swear off any cow byproducts. And that was what Rochelle was, thick, not sloppy thick but firm "damn that girl is built" thick. Sporting measurements of 38d, 24, and 38 at just 5'5, she had enough ass to feed an entire Rwandan village.

I 'm not into women or anything, but I have to admit she is beautiful. Looking like Sana'a Lathan wasn't the only thing she was going for her. Unlike most of us follicle challenged sistas, she had hair going down to that big ass of hers due to her Native American heritage. Even as she adjusted her makeup in a compact mirror, I wondered how she managed to get away with wearing revealing clothes in her line of work. Post office attire doesn't exactly scream sexy.

But I got to give my girl props because she knew how to pull it off. She knew how to make postal blue look stunning. Her short sleeve shirt was unbuttoned low enough to show off the perky breast she was blessed with. And the super short navy blue skort she wore was high enough to show off the black of her ass. I hated that she had a nice body while all I had was a pretty face. They called me "olive oil" for a reason in college.

I've known Rochelle for nearly seventeen years, we shared an apartment together in Harlem when we both attended F.I.T. During that point in my life I lived, day by day. Now I've taken a different road, the road that leads to God. Moral cleanliness is the code I live by; I've given my life to the lord. I attend church with my fiancé every Sunday and feel content to wait until my marriage day when he can part my legs like Moses parted the red sea.

I'm even particular about what I put in my body. I'm a flexitarian, the fancy word to describe those few people that eat a mostly vegetarian diet, but occasionally indulge in meat eating

Truth be told, even though I've made numerous strides in my life, I'm far from perfect. I don't attend church more than once a week and there is never a passing day when I don't use some type of foul language. Not to mention that I'm a workaholic in love with the finer things my low six-figure salary provides. Titus always says that if I let go of material things god will *give* me all the necessities of life. But in all the times I've looked down at the feet of the women in his congregation, I've never noticed a pair of

Christian Louboutin's. Therefore, I might as well continue to work for my necessities.

"You are definitely better than me. As gorgeous as Titus is, I would be in jail for rape already."

I had to admit being engaged to a Minister came with its disadvantages. I respected my fiancé Reverend Titus Rosemond, but we dated for over two years and he had yet to lay a solitary finger on me. I mean I am fine as hell so I know it's not from lack of visual stimulation. Yet even on those rare occasions when we're alone, things never got heated up. Hell, they didn't even get Lukewarm. For once, a man respected me and I hated it.

"Rochelle, you need to get your mind out the gutter. From what you tell me about Dexter, I know your sex life isn't all what it's cracked up to be either. You need to start going to church with me," I said.

Rochelle has been married for ten years. Yet she spent more time in my guest room than she did in her own bed. It represents all that is wrong in this world when women marry men with more inches on their penis than dollars in their pocket.

"Dexter ain't the only one man out there that's getting' this nana," she said while applying lip-gloss to her lips.

I gave her *the look*. She wasn't stupid enough to cheat on jealous ass Dexter. He worked for the N.Y.P.D as a police officer and was known to monitor her. Last year he had a detective friend of his follow her because he *thought* she was cheating. It turned out she was only planning his birthday. And that wasn't the crazy part; he damn near killed the mailman after catching him leaving the apartment after Rochelle signed for a package. I could only imagine what he'd do if she really was sleeping around.

"Rochelle, don't play with me," I warned, taking another sip of my frappuccino.

"Do I look like I'm playing?" she said taking out an opened box of condoms from her knock off Gucci purse.

During the weekdays, early in the morning, the mall served as a place to jog for some in the community. However, Rochelle didn't give two fucks that some of the men were nearly breaking their necks to stare at her once she revealed that condom box. Hating to cause a scene, I snatched them from her fingertips and put them under my left leg.

"You want to sign your death certificate? What if Dexter found these?" I reasoned.

"And if he did, forget him," she replied dismissively waving her hands. "I got more where those came from. And you do notice those are XXL condoms. Dexter ain't fitting into those."

I sucked my teeth, removed a strand of hair from my eyes and swept biscotti crumbs from off my lap. It was always some new drama in her life. We commuted together from Manhattan to Paramus, New Jersey and every morning it was the same shit. Rochelle wasn't content unless she was fighting with Dexter. Sometimes it felt as if she was addicted to makeup sex.

Dexter was jealous and broke, but he treated her like gold and took care of the child she had from a previous relationship. Not to mention he had done the unthinkable and put a ring on her finger. It took me all of thirty-four years before a man considered me marriage material. What Rochelle should do is take a look at the statistics for unmarried sistas.

However ghetto she may seem, the girl is smart as hell, but her kryptonite has always been thugs. That's why she had to drop out after sophomore year at F.I.T, because of some lame ass brotha with much game, much dick, but not enough sense. She ended up rearing his child while he sat in a cell doing twenty-five to life in Rikers.

Still, Unique, my godson, was the best thing that could've happened to her. When he was born he looked like his father and was just as bad, but he provided her with some semblance of stability. No one could ever accuse Rochelle of not being a great mother, and that's why she's so heart broken. When you can't give a child materially what they want, they sometimes feel like they have to do it on their own. Unique was gunned down last year at seventeen as he robbed a check-cashing place, leaving behind his mother's crushed heart and a son that bore his name.

That's why I look the other way as she battles an early midlife crisis. Once Unique was laid to rest, it was like her good sense was buried with him. Now, she acted as if he was never born, and buried her pain by hitting up clubs and using my guest room as her alibi. Sometimes it felt as though she had regressed to that Nineteen-year-old girl that she was when her son was born.

Once upon a time, I was no better than Rochelle. Just because I'm gonna be a minister's wife didn't mean I was an angel. My body needed the rest since I'd taken a vow of celibacy four years ago. Back in the day if a man with a great smile, a nice car and a hefty bank account even looked my way, I spread my legs. Now I respect myself, even though I still reap the regrets of my promiscuous past and I hope Rochelle would do the same.

"By the way, Angelica, you mean to tell me that you're wearing those short shorts and you're not expecting niggas to holla."

I took an inventory of my gear. My khaki short shorts did put a spotlight on my long caramel legs. But I only wore them because they went well with my brown Jimmy Choo bucket bag and the pair of sling backs on my feet.

"I don't need to impress anyone. I got a man."

"You mean, a man not giving you any of that funky stuff."

She laughed as she stood, bending over the table and pulling at my brown pomegranate print camisole. "I gotta get to work, but I suggest that you cover up those tatas and put on some pants if you don't want these trifling niggas hitting on you."

Monday's are always especially busy. I worked in the Grand State Plaza Mall. As the contemporary sportswear buyer for Neiman Marcus, I barely found time for lunch. Sometimes I could just scream at all the tasks that had to be accomplished before closing. Between checking the sales reports, setting up displays, dressing mannequins, doing sample fittings and meeting with vendors, I barely had enough time for myself or my man. Not to mention that in two days my man was going away for three weeks on a missionary mission to Africa and I was going to have to plan all the tedious details of our wedding alone.

I knew the wedding plans would take all of my free time, if not more. While looking down at my desk, I remember to finalize the details with my Wedding Planner. With my final fitting schedules two weeks from now, the last thing on my mind was food. Even though I was 5'7 and a fit 126lbs I wanted to make sure, I could at least *fit* into my dress.

As I looked at the hands on my three thousand dollar Cartier San demoiselle watch, which read 4:09pm, I realized I had better call my wedding planner, Marcellus, before he was gone for the day.

"Hello, Suri wedding planning, Marcellus speaking," Marcellus said in his knockoff French accent. I wasn't hating on him, but he knew damn well he came from Harlem. Nothing against gay men, but dealing with Marcellus was like dealing with another woman. I noticed that about him as we set the menu for my wedding. Don't tell him he's wrong about something or he'll read you up and down, right to left like a real diva would. It's a damn shame that a tall, dark, chocolate brotha like him decided to switch team.

"Hi darling! This is Angelica Thompson."

"I'm glad you called mademoiselle. I just called the Reverend. I apologize for the discrepancy."

"What discrepancy?" I wanted to hide the concern in my voice but it was too late.

"You didn't get my message? The caterer double booked on the date of your wedding."

"And what does that mean?"

"They won't have the man power to cater your wedding. The other event was scheduled first."

"Because of their incompetence I have to suffer."

"Missy, they will issue a total refund of the monies paid back to you." I could sense the trepidation in his voice. I knew their game, someone with more money and importance had offered the caterer a better deal. I didn't mean to take my anger out on Marcellus, but he did recommend the caterer.

"How am I gonna find a damn caterer to cater *my* wedding a month before. I'm not serving cheese and crackers, you know." I got up and closed the door to my office, because I knew things were only going to get worse.

"I know someone that would take the account, missy."

"If you call me missy again, I'm gonna jump through this phone and choke the life out of you."

"I know you're angry, but I can recommend a great caterer for you."

"Why would I want to deal with anyone that you recommend? You did insist on the first one. And look at the situation I'm stuck in," I snapped.

"It's the least I can do due to the incompetence of the caterer's secretary," he tried cleaning up the caterer's mistake. I hated when people passed along their failures to insubordinates.

"The least they can do is send back my money for the wedding pronto or *you* both will be hearing from my lawyer."

"The Reverend was very understanding when I explained the situation. I don't understand the problem."

"You mean the groom. Did he sit down with you and go over the seating arrangements."

"No," he mumbled.

"Did he go over the menu or does he even know the type of fabric I want on the cocktail tables?"

"No," he answered in an exasperated tone.

"So why would you call him before me?" I asked

Who was he to call my fiancé? Titus had no goddamn say when it came to *my* wedding. It was going to be *my* show he was just my co-star. Marcellus knew better than asking a man to do what clearly took the precise planning and meticulous detailed touch of a woman. That's why I decided to have a small wedding party, only my maid of honor and Titus' best man would be standing front and center. It didn't make sense to have a large party of people whose sole purpose in attending would be to outshine the bride and find their next sexual conquest. No one was going to steal my shine.

Marcellus didn't have anything else to say and I didn't even care for an answer. I slammed the phone down even though I had a lot more choice words for that wannabe French asshole. A month before my wedding and things were already coming apart. Maybe it was a sign.

I fought the urge to pinch Titus butt cheeks as he prepared to roll a strike at the Chelsea Pier Lanes. For a brotha, he had a nice, cute, sumtin anotha happening in the back of his Levis. He made me want to do more than shout. But I was content to stare from a distance. I hated our dates; they were always so…casual and not romantic. Like usual, I was stuck twiddling my thumbs under the glow of the dark disco lights as a bunch of lame elderly people in the next booth did the hot potato. And the smell of the hotdogs Titus ordered had me on the verge of throwing up. I didn't eat meat, not unless you count dick.

Slowly, but surely I was beginning to lose the conviction I had when I started my vow of celibacy. In the beginning it was easy because in my last relationship I got hurt so bad I didn't want any part of a man. After putting my blood, sweat and tears into a relationship with a married man, I was left feeling lower than low. I didn't even take the time to think that since he was cheating on his wife, cheating on me wasn't out of the question. Thinking back, the realization of his deception angered me so much that I didn't want to see another naked brotha for fear that I would catch a flashback and cut off some innocent mans penis because of the unfaithfulness of another.

My naiveté got the better of me four years ago. Since then, I've learned not to take every man at his word. That's exactly why I was happy to have found someone like Titus. Sex comes a dime a dozen. But a faithful man, not to mention a man that is still a virgin is something to be treasured. Of course, my feelings for Titus weren't love at first sight, even though he's fine, but I know that *someday* I'll love him.

Titus took a bite from his hot dog as he sat across from me. He was casually dressed in a pair of black Prada slacks I bought him and a short sleeved v-neck t-shirt. His great abs and muscular arms looked great in anything. And he knew it; though he was a man of god he was still a man and felt confident about his.

I appreciated a man with great taste. I appreciated fine things in general and Titus was able to provide me with the life I deserved. Not only was he the highly esteemed leader of his own non-denominational church, but an in demand motivational speaker. Last year alone, he made well over seven figures and had also paid the mortgage on my Tribeca condominium. Though he lived in a modest one-bedroom basement apartment in Harlem, his pockets were deep.

"Angelica, what's bothering you? Is the situation with the caterer still on your mind?" he asked with sincerity in his emerald eyes. I'd long forgotten about the caterer hours ago. That wasn't my problem. I despised the fact that Titus never sat next to me or displayed any signs of affection. When I revealed my concerns once before, he told me that the devil was clouding my judgment.

"You know I love you. But sometimes I feel like you're not even into me," I whispered. Having come from where I came from, I hated wearing any emotion on my sleeves.

"I love you too and I'm here with you. But what are you exactly asking me?" He moved his food to the side, wiped his gorgeous mouth and hands with a napkin and moved his chair closer. But not close enough.

"Do you ever want me?"

"My love for you far surpasses any physical act, if that is where you're getting at."

"But how do you know I can please you?" I wondered. His jaws clenched and his eyelids narrowed. Lines began to form on his head and I knew I had frustrated him.

"I'm beginning to wonder why that's always an issue. You've supposedly waited thirty-four years and you mean to tell me you can't wait another month. Should I be worried while I'm away doing the lord's work?" His tone had sharpened, as if he was talking to a wayward member of his congregation.

Lying can be deadly. It also fills one with guilt. That night two years ago in the Onyx lounge as we talked, he asked me one question. How long have you maintained your cleanliness before god? I answered since birth. I told him that I would never give myself to a man unless he was my husband. He believed me, at that time I needed him to. Now I wished I never lied.

But I needed to impress him. Coming from a long line of Ministers and clergymen, he was shielded from the bitter world I had to face. In his closed circle of family members, I would've been considered a sinner. He said he knew I was his wife. And I needed to be viewed as someone who was worth more than lying on her back.

"I just want a kiss," I humbly confessed.

Wasn't I to be desired? I hated putting on an act for him and everyone else who expected more out of the prospective wife of a minister. Even my baggy, pink velour jumpsuit concealed everything I had to offer. If Titus had seen my outfit earlier, he'd damn near have had a heart attack. But no, I had to dress modest, wear dresses down near my ankles and always act like I was on some unreachable spiritual plain. Why, because I was a minister's fiancé?

Titus always carried a leather carrying case. It was an old beat up looking bag from when he was a child singing on the choir in his father's church. The Velcro had long ago stopped catching and when he carried it, he always had to hold it under his arm to keep it closed. As he opened his antique bag, I instantly knew what to expect. He extracted his black bound bible, turned to his appointed scripture and put on his Cartier reading glasses, in the middle of a crowded bowling alley. Like usual, he couldn't tell me from his own words why he couldn't touch me.

"Let me read you something from…"

I stood in the front pew of Mount Bethel A.M.E listening to my man give another heart wrenching Eulogy for one of his beloved Deacons, Deacon Marshall who was also City Councilman . I held hands with the widow, trying my best to provide her with much needed strength as she stared at the lifeless body of her husband in the bronze colored coffin only a few feet away. She shook her head as Titus spoke and fought back tears with a white handkerchief.

Trying her best to be the pillar of strength for her family, she would reveal a contrived smile whenever Titus made a joke to lighten the mood. At least he fortified her through candid reflections. All I could do was lean over and whisper in her ear "The lord will not fail you." Those words meant nothing to me, they just sounded like the right thing to say at this particular time.

Looking down from the altar into the eyes of Sister Marshall he said, "Your husband's in a better place. A place where his step has more spring, his legs more pep and where his love for you will never perish. Your love was a perfect love that distance, time and death could never stop. It's persevering. And the day you meet again, its radiance will not have dimmed. But it will be even more omnipotent."

Those words touched her, made her smile with fervor while crying tears of joy. Titus was always eloquent when speaking from the pulpit. Titus loved his congregation and held a self-sacrificing affection for them that he never showed me. For that reason, I was jealous of the attention he gave. If anyone were missing, he would call him or her personally. If anyone seemed down, he would impart words of encouragement, and if anyone were in need, he would provide food, both spiritual and physical.

However, he ignored who was supposed to be the most important component in his life. His congregation was his first love and I felt like a mistress.

Befitting of the mood, rain began to pelt the tinted limousine window as we drove from the burial site. We were alone, yet the silence we held had become customary in our courtship. We dated for two years without ever really talking. Our engagement was only common routine. It wasn't even spectacular, not over a candle light dinner and he didn't surprise me by getting on bended knee in front of friends and family. It was over the phone as we read the bible together.

The interior lights were on, Titus was reading from his bible, caught in the private recesses of his psyche he never let anyone near him. Everyone had another side, but his was well hidden and bolted shut with an impenetrable lock

I don't know what I was supposed to look for in a soul mate. My record of boyfriends would attest to the fact that I habitually pick no good men. It wasn't as if I had a father around to compare them to. Thus, I relied on my instincts, which were fickle to say the least. I tried the thug thing, the baller thing, even tried the white thing until I found out the myth about the size of their members was really a fair assessment. Titus on the other hand was the only honorable male to ever lay eyes on me. And I didn't want to lose a man who had saved himself all his life for me.

"Did you speak to Sister Marshall before you left?" Titus asked.

"I didn't get a chance to," I said. In reality, there was nothing for me to say, I didn't know her and better yet, I didn't know her husband. "I wasn't having one of my better nights."

"You have to make it an obligation. My congregation looks to you for inspiration. You can't have an off night. When we get to her house, make it a point to speak with her"

There were many things he said I couldn't do. I couldn't curse, couldn't hang with the wrong crowd a definition, which all of my friends fell under and I couldn't go out on the town. In all actuality, he didn't want me to be me.

I powered down the back window. Without fresh air, I was beginning to get carsick. "I need to get home. I got work in the morning and I think I'm coming down with something," I said, lying on both accounts.

"You can go to work and slave for people with low moral fiber, but you can't give support to a widow." He shook his head, took his eyes out of the bible, leaned in his seat and crossed his legs. "Until you put the work of the lord first, your job situation will never improve."

"I put the lord first," I said raising my voice.

"Then the job must go."

This man didn't realize how much I'd already sacrificed for him, for his love. Four years earlier, I sinned vehemently on a regular basis. I would stay out into the early morning, dabble in about every party drug imaginable and fornicate like it was going out of style. That life style came with a price. Forget baby momma drama, I had nigga's wife strife. Titus just didn't know that what attracted me to him more than his bank account and good looks was his baggage free life.

"Titus, you don't hear me telling you to leave the church."

"That makes no sense and you know it. This isn't a career; it's a calling and a privilege. I've worked diligently to get where I am. And until the lord tells me to stop, this is where I'll remain."

"Exactly, so why would you ask me to quit something I worked hard for?"

He hated when I went against him. I could hear his teeth grind and see his jaw lock. My defiance was killing him inside. He was old school, from a Mid-western Baptist family where women were seen, but not heard. I met his mother, Marjorie when we went to visit his family in Arkansas and could tell she had never made a worthwhile decision in all forty years of marriage. His father was unimpressive physically; barely standing an inch above his five foot four-inch wife, but was still domineering. She jumped when he spoke, making it her divine function to care for his unrealistic preferences. I detested the way he treated her and to make things worse, I had to stay in Titus' childhood bedroom as he slept in a nearby hotel. This meant I had to bear with his Father's chauvinistic ways alone.

During my stay, a snowstorm hit and dumped a foot of slush on the ground. When I awoke in the morning to the sound of a shovel scrapping against gravel, I was surprised to see Marjorie in her robe and boots waist deep in a mound of snow making sure not to scrape the shovel against her husband's Cadillac.

Titus, though, wasn't his father. He wasn't a domineering man, but didn't take after his mother either. He was sort of in the middle. I guess that's what two parents are for. Besides, he couldn't get away doing to me what his father did to his mother.

"I wished you could come with me on my missionary trip," he said, trying to turn on his natural charm.

"You can't blame my job for that," I said stretching my right hand out and showing off my ring.

"Maybe not in this instance, but there will be other times," he said.

"Hopefully those will be few and far between," I responded.

The car came to a halt outside the front door of my building. I wanted to jump across the seat and put my lips against his, but it wouldn't do any good. His chastity meant too much to him, even more than my happiness.

"Well, my heart. Guess this is goodbye for the next three weeks," he said softly. He winked at me, with glazed over eyes. Obviously, our time apart weighed on his mind.

I composed myself, waited for the driver to get out and open my door. I looked in my little compact mirror, made sure my makeup looked flawless, even though it was not like I had done anything to mess it up.

"Can you join me for breakfast in the morning, I'm cooking. I'll appreciate it if you'd join me for a feast in the morning," I stated as the driver let the cool summer breeze in as he opened the door. I had never cooked in my life, didn't have a mother to teach me. My breakfast of champions consisted of a hot cup of coffee and a pastry both store bought. I tried making coffee once and ended up with something that looked like used car oil. However, I did not want him to leave like this. Besides, he never hid the fact that he wanted a domestic wife. Maybe I could cook my way into getting that elusive first kiss.

"If you're cooking, I'm there. I think that is a great idea. I'll be there with an empty stomach," he rejoiced. With a huge smile on his face, he blew me a kiss as I stepped out onto the sidewalk. I blew him one in return, praying to receive the real thing to hold me over in his absence.

As the fire detector sounded, I rushed into the living room and opened the windows, put the fan atop the gas range on high and continued to cook. I flipped the sausage over, couldn't tell whether it was done, it felt frozen to the touch but had a crispy black coat on each side. Since I prepared eggs before hand, the residue left behind had turned a licorice color, making it difficult to make the sausage look golden brown as it did on the package.

The oven timer went off. My buttermilk biscuits were done; I opened the oven door and smiled as I beheld my creation. They looked light and fluffy, the tops were brownish yellow and the sides were a light yellow. I put on the brand new pair of oven mitts I never used and took them out the oven. After placing the pan atop the plastic that covered my kitchen table, I grabbed the spatula from the frying pan where I was cooking the sausage and used it to pry the biscuits from the pan. The bottoms were baked to the pan, so I cut off the good part and soaked the pan along with the bottoms in the sink. Putting the finishing touches on breakfast, I set a place for Titus at my dining room table and lit an apple crisp candle to further entice his taste buds.

I looked at the clock, it was nearly eight and Titus told me he'd be here by that time. My suit for work was already laid out, but I decided to put on a sexy pair of pajamas I bought at La Perla instead. They weren't overtly revealing, but if he looked, close enough his eyes could behold my tantalizing curves. This would be the first time we were alone, so I wanted to make access as easy as possible without going all out and answering the door in the nude.

Taking off my robe in front of my mirror, I pinched a finger full of fat from my waist. My body wasn't in tiptop shape like I wanted it to be, thus I was going to have to cut the pastries from my diet. I didn't want Titus to be traumatized the first time he saw a naked woman. Jogging would definitely be on the menu for the weekend.

I rubbed Donna Karen's gold body lotion all over, sprayed Victoria secret vanilla lace body spray on my breasts and privates and slipped into my purple silk PJ's.

I heard a light knock at my door and couldn't restrain my smile. Titus made me feel like the luckiest woman on earth. There's nothing like the feeling that overtakes you when you make your man a home cooked meal. Wonder why I hadn't tried it earlier. Seeing the smile on his face while he dived into my food would be the ultimate compliment.

Like a real woman, I took my time to answer the door, wanted him to be good and eager when he saw me. I whistled as I sashayed down the hallway leading to my foyer and was taken aback when I peeked through the peephole and saw who was outside of my door. There was nothing wrong with Titus; he looked good dressed in one of his tailored suits bearing flowers and a smile. But it was who he brought along that concerned me and instantly killed any thoughts I had of seducing him.

"Hi. How are you doing, Sister Mathews?" I said opening the door and forcing a smile as Sister Mathews walked by me without as much as a glance.

Sister Mathews was one of the founding members of Mount Bethel A.M.E. She was in her seventies, with a polka dot face, saggy titties and a bad attitude. I sensed from our first meeting that she wished that one of her dog-faced daughters were in my shoes. Ever since my engagement, she's done everything in her power to spite me. This was the icing on the cake. I didn't understand why she hated me. Titus shared a phone line with her and sometimes when I call, she'll hang up and blame it on her sleeping pills. However, part of me felt like she had me pegged, knew my game and understood that in this day and age it was almost impossible to be a virgin. I could tell it in her deciphering stares whenever I wore something less than modest in church. A younger woman has no chance against an older woman. And surely, she had been there, seen it and probably done everything I had not so long ago. No woman married for more than forty years has a shortage of tricks up her sleeves and that's why I feared her.

"It looks great in here," Titus said shaking my hand as he stepped into my apartment for the first time. He had been in my building many times but never made the trek upstairs.

I closed the door and shook my head as Titus walked ahead. I anticipated a morning I would never forget and at that moment, I was sure of it.

Sister Mathews walked around my kitchen poking her face into every pot on top of my stove with a disgusted look.

"You've done some serious cooking in here." Titus said admiring the bowls of food on the granite countertops island.

"It also smells like she's done some serious burning as well," Sister Mathews retorted. That had Titus tickled, laughing like he needed an anti-laugh antidote.

"Well, Mama Mathews, the lord says waste not want not." Titus laughed taking her coat and placing a kiss on her cheek as she took a seat.

She held her purse in front of her; clutching it with both gloved hands like someone was gonna rob her. She wore a pink church dress that looked like it was made from cactus-like material and a huge hat adorned the matted gray naps that peeked from her black wig. The hat was pink linen as well with a lavender matte and a satin sash and bow.

"Put me down for the want not and a cup of tea," she said, staring at me as if I was her maid or something. Titus left the room and went into the living room so he could put her coat away along with his.

Like a Christian woman, I bit my tongue and asked, "I have an assortment. Do you prefer Lipton or Chai?"

"You got any Earl Grey? I got a taste for some Earl Grey," she said.

"No, only Lipton and Chai," I said with a plastic smile.

"I don't want any then. What is an assortment of tea without Earl Grey?" she said in a huffed tone.

"I can go to the store if you want."

"I'm sure you wouldn't mind if I went to the store," she said staring at me suspiciously.

"What was that?" I asked shocked by her accusation.

"No God fearing woman asks a man to come alone to her home if she has something holy in mind. You may have Titus fooled, but you're a harlot and will eventually be cast out of the lord's house," she pointed her finger rigidly in my direction making her position clearly understood.

"I don't know why you would doubt my intentions for him. I would never hurt him. But it should be of no concern to you either way, he will be my husband," I said coyly with a hint of sarcasm.

"What sinners keep in the dark, the lord brings to the light," she said as Titus walked into the kitchen, stood between us and grabbed our hands.

"Before we enjoy this meal, let's bow our heads..." Titus said with closed eyes. I didn't close mine, neither did Sister Mathews, we locked eyes and didn't budge until he said Amen.

Ignoring the battle-axe, I fixed Titus' plate, put the white roses he bought for me in a vase and sat next to him as he tried to enjoy my food. He didn't like it all that well and I knew it from the time he bit into an eggshell, but he played the role of the appreciative fiancé and didn't complain. I thanked him for that.

"This was great food," Titus said as he broke off a piece of frozen sausage with his fork.

"Tell the truth, don't spare me. It was terrible, wasn't it?" I asked.

"It was pretty bad," he admitted putting his arms around my shoulders, touching me for the first time in a romantic way.

I pursed out my lips and with puppy dog eyes playfully sobbed, "Now you see why I don't cook."

"And the world's a better place because of it," Sister Mathews stuck her two cents in. "I taught my daughters as soon as they came out the womb how to make a decent meal. It makes no sense for a married woman to not know her way around the kitchen. I say the kitchen and bedroom go hand in hand. That's why my husband, God rest his soul, had no reason to be any other place but home. In my household, I made it a priority that my daughters know how to make a man happy." She put her wrinkled hands across the table and placed them on top of Titus's. Luckily, I did not have a knife or fork at my disposal or I would have gladly crippled her.

I wanted to say something back for once, give her a taste of her own medicine, but could not since Titus thought of her as a second mother. He lived in the basement apartment of her brownstone and she always made sure to cook him three meals a day.

I could also tell she wanted a reason to berate my apartment as she looked around, but I kept my place tidy. If anything, I knew how to clean.

"I don't know what I'm gonna do when you leave," I said staring into Titus' green eyes while he sipped a glass of orange juice.

"You won't be the only one feeling lost," he said. Our faces were only inches apart, the impassioned look in his eyes told me to make my move, regardless of Sister Mathews Judgmental gaze. We moved closer, I closed my eyes. Prepared my lips to touch his, relaxed my tongue in hopes that it would intertwine with his. However, a loud gag got my attention. It sounded like someone was choking. I opened my eyes to see Titus get up from his seat and rush over to Sister Mathews.

She was keeled over looking like she was gonna spit out a lung. Titus rubbed her back and tapped it softly.

"Get me a glass of water!" he ordered me.

I went to the faucet, drew some cold tap water in a glass and handed it to him. She wasn't worth wasting Evian on. Titus held the glass to her lips as she brought her head back. She drunk from it, caught her breath and sighed intensely as if she was underwater for twenty minutes.

"Mama Mathews, are you alright," he said with concern.

"I neglected to take my medicine," she said as he hugged her.

"Okay mama, I'll get your coat," he said retreating to the living room.

"Top that, Jezebel!" she said with a wink.

They left minutes later, leaving behind not only dishes, but also the realization that maybe I was taking on more than I could bear, because when I marry Titus I marry his church as well.

Sample chapter from

My partner's Wife

By

Michael Glenn Yates

Chapter 4

Something was wrong, out of place. Marcus was surrounded by complete darkness as he shut the door behind him and stood inside his girlfriend's apartment. The shades were drawn, shutting out the late evening sunlight. Tamala usually allowed the sunshine in to 'feed' her plants as she would say, so it was strange for her apartment to be this dark at this time of day. Marcus allowed his eyes to adjust before moving away from the closed door. Just as he was fumbling along the wall for a light switch, he heard several muffled thumps coming from one of the rooms off of the darkened hallway just to the right of him.

It sounded as if someone was in a struggle or fight. Marcus's police instincts took over as he slowly walked in the direction of the barely audible noise. He heard a slap followed quickly by a woman's scream. *Tamala!* His heart nearly lept out of his chest and his muscles tightened in his body as fear and stress filled him. Marcus thought about running toward the scream but decided against it. In Marcus's line of work rushing into a circumstance could get an officer killed, and the person he intended on helping. Trusting in that knowledge now was crucial. He had the element of surprise on his side; catching the burglar or intruder unawares was the best course of action.

Once again another one of Tamala's screams drifted from the darkened confines of the hallway. The gift he was carrying fell silently to the carpet as Marcus instinctively reached for his right side searching for a gun that was not there. A cop wears a gun day-in and day-out so it becomes second nature to grab for it when he feels threatened. Marcus remembered that he was not wearing his gun given he was in a tuxedo. For a brief moment, he experienced indecision. It was too dark to try to find Tamala's telephone, which had probably been ripped out of the wall by the home invaders. Turning on a light would alert the intruders to his presence. He thought about turning around to retrieve his cell phone, which was in his car, but he just could not leave Tamala alone with whoever was assaulting her.

Marcus realized that he had no choice but to confront whoever was hurting Tamala. Fear seeped deep within him as he continued walking toward the noise, which grew louder as he stepped into the short hallway. Saving the love of his life was his only concern.

***

Marcus heard the grunting and moaning before he even got to Tamala's master bedroom. Faint candlelight spilled out from the largest of two bedrooms and into the dimly lit hallway. Feeling his heart in his throat and finding it very hard to breath, Marcus slowly walked toward the doorway hoping against hope that he was not hearing what he thought he was hearing. As he stood to the side of the doorway with sweat dripping down his baldpate, he heard not only grunts and panting, but also desire, passion, and wantonness.

As his heart dropped, Marcus tried to listen to the unmistakable sound of his impending fiancée's breathless voice drifting from the candlelit bedroom, *"It's yours damit…ahh-ahhhhhhhh…*it's *yoursssss*! Lamarrrrr…oh, fuck, it's soooo good! Oh, GOD…yeessss, like that, don't stop! YESSSS that's it, BABY! My pus...my pussy is yoursssss! *Smack my ass again*!"

(SMACK)

"Oh, GOD, Lamar. I love that shit!" Then Marcus heard a sound that had become commonplace to him over the last two years...the sound of Tamala reaching her sexual peak, her climax.

Mere seconds later, Marcus heard a man's voice, "I'm comin'....*shit*, girl...TAKE-MY-SHIT...oooooh. FUCK, ooooooooooooooh FUCK...DAMN, GIRLLLLLLLL! You got, you got some damn...*damn* good pussy, Tamala!"

Then Marcus heard them shifting on the waterbed, the water sloshing from their spent pleasure. The sound of heavy breathing then kissing reached him. The strong smell of sex wafted from the bedroom out into the hallway where Marcus stood against the wall, in total shock. Now the male voice said softly, "Tamala, ya *pussy* really is da bomb." The couple giggled at the latter comment. After what seemed like the longest pause in history, Marcus heard the lovers whispering sweet things, intimate things...things that only lovers share after a great session of sex.

He could almost see Tamala's sexy light brown eyes, her short brown wavy hair, very soft to the touch, her perky round breasts with supple pink nipples, her plump buttocks, and her 5-foot, 110-pound, petite frame lying there sweaty and entangled with her...with her co-conspirator, her lover.

Marcus just stood there, stood there in the hallway with the back of his baldhead pressed against the wall, eyes closed, listening to their intimate whispering. He seemed almost catatonic, frozen where he stood close to that open bedroom door, and a few feet from the couple. He felt as if he was in a bad dream, actually a nightmare. He sighed quietly then opened his eyes. Candlelight continued to flicker into the hallway. Unconsciously, he began to finger the ring case in his right pants pocket. After a few minutes of staring into space, he simply tiptoed out of Tamala's apartment like a defeated basketball player leaving the hardwood court after missing the winning shot in the championship game.

The dejected off-duty cop, unable to confront the reality that the lady of his life was intimate with another man, left the apartment, shutting the door gently behind him. Marcus knew that he was not a saint. In fact, he had cheated in the past on ex-girlfriends, but never on his loving Tamala. She was his world, his everything! The brightness of the sun blinded him as he slowly made his way back down the stairs.

As Marcus reached the ground level, he saw the black polished limo, gleaming in the fading sunlight, parked in front of the apartment complex blocking a row of cars. The driver was wiping down the already shiny limousine with a clean white rag. Marcus walked over to the older, heavyset black man dressed in a nice tux, probably not rented, and dismissed him. He swallowed back tears of pain and rage. Marcus decided to take solace in going to work. Policing was the only way to keep his confused mind away from his latest plight.

My Partners Wife

In this twisted tale of seduction, Marcus Williams finds himself taking refuge in the arms of a woman completely forbidden to him after he discovered his cheating □iancée s sexual trysts. His life spirals out of control after the death of his partner while the killer is still on the loose. Marcus is conflicted about his decision to honor his partner or to completely allow his heart to decide his fate. Always the sucker for love, Marcus starts to fall head over heels for his partner s wife. However, with more deaths on the horizon, Marcus may soon find himself serving time with the same convicts he had been putting behind bars.

In Stores!!

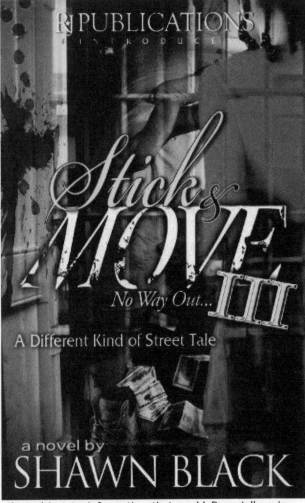

Serosa becomes the subject to information that could financially ruin and possibly destroy the lives and careers of many prominent people involved in the government if this data is exposed. As this intricate plot thickens, speculations start mounting and a whirlwind of death, deceit, and betrayal finds its way into the ranks of a once impenetrable core of the government. Will Serosa fall victim to the genetic structure that indirectly binds her to her parents causing her to realize there s NO WAY OUT!

In Stores!!!

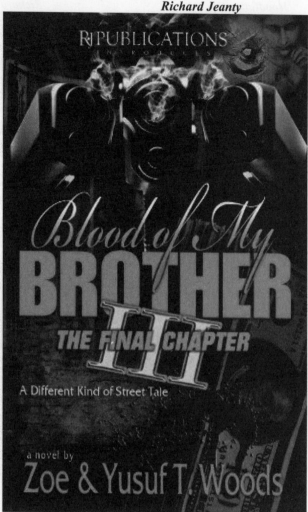

Retiring is no longer an option for Roc, who is now forced to restudy Philly's vicious streets through blood filled eyes. He realizes that his brother's killer is none other than his mentor, Mr. Holmes. With this knowledge, the strategic game of chess that began with the pushing of a pawn in the Blood of My Brother series, symbolizes one of love, loyalty, blood, mayhem, and death. In the end, the streets of Philadelphia will never be the same...

In Storess!!!

After Chasin' Satisfaction, Julius finds that satisfaction is not all that it's cracked up to be. It left nothing but death in its aftermath. Now living the glamorous life in Miami while putting the finishing touches on his hybrid condo hotel, he realizes with newfound success he's now become the hunted. Julian's success is threatened as someone from his past vows revenge on him.

In Stores!!!

It may not be Histeria Lane, but these desperate housewives are fed up with their neglecting husbands. Their sexual needs take precedence over the millions of dollars their husbands bring home every year to keep them happy in their affluent neighborhood. While their husbands claim to be hard at work, these wives are doing a little work of their own with the bedroom bandit. Is the bandit swift enough to evade these angry husbands?

In Stores!!

NEGLECTED SOULS

Motherhood and the trials of loving too hard and not enough frame this story...The realism of these characters will bring tears to your spirit as you discover the hero in the villain you never saw coming...

In Stores!!!

Jimmy and Nina continue to feel a void in their lives because they haven't a clue about their genealogical make-up. Jimmy falls victims to a life threatening illness and only the right organ donor can save his life. Will the donor be the bridge to reconnect Jimmy and Nina to their biological family? Will Nina be the strength for her brother in his time of need? Will they ever find out what really happened to their mother?

In Stores!!!

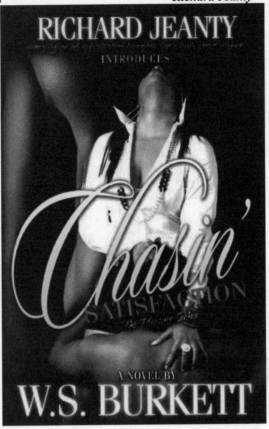

Betrayal, lust, lies, murder, deception, sex and tainted love frame this story... Julian Stevens lacks the ambition and freak ability that Miko looks for in a man, but she married him despite his flaws to spite an ex-boyfriend. When Miko least expects it, the old boyfriend shows up and ready to sweep her off her feet again. She wants to have her cake and eat it too. While Miko's doing her own thing, Julian is determined to become everything Miko ever wanted in a man and more, but will he go to extreme lengths to prove he's worthy of Miko's love? Julian Stevens soon finds out that he's capable of being more than he could ever imagine as he embarks on a journey that will change his life forever.

In Stores!!!

The police in New York and other major cities around the country are increasingly victimizing black men. The violence has escalated to deadly force, most of the time without justification. In this controversial book, noted author Richard Jeanty, tackles the problem of police brutality and the unfair treatment of Black men at the hands of police in New York City and the rest of the country.

In Stores!!!

Just when Darren thinks his relationship with Tina is flourishing, there is yet another hurdle on the road hindering their bliss. Tina saw a therapist for months to deal with her sexual addiction, but now Darren is wondering if she was ever treated completely. Darren has not been taking care of home and Tina's frustrated and agrees to a break-up with Darren. Will Darren lose Tina for good? Will Tina ever realize that Darren is the best man for her?

In Stores!!

Ronald Murphy was a player all his life until he and his best friend, Myles, met the women of their dreams during a brief vacation in South Beach, Florida. Sexual Jeopardy is story of trust, betrayal, forgiveness, friendship and hope.

In Stores!!!

A NEW NOVEL FROM THE AUTHOR OF "NEGLECTED SOULS" AND "MEETING MS. RIGHT"

RICHARD JEANTY

SEXUAL
exploits of a
NYMPHO

" The book is hotter, steamier and sexier
than the title suggests. Jeanty has done it again."
–Treasure E. Blue Essence best selling author of
Harlem Girl Lost

Tina develops an insatiable sexual appetite very early in life. She only loves her boyfriend, Darren, but he's too far away in college to satisfy her sexual needs.

Tina decides to get buck wild away in college

Will her sexual trysts jeopardize the lives of the men in her life?

In Stores!!!

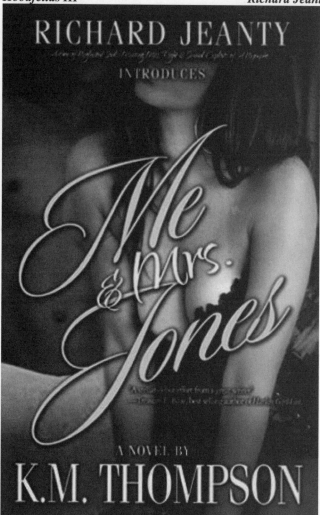

Faith Jones, a woman in her mid-thirties, has given up on ever finding love again until she met her son's best friend, Darius. Faith Jones is walking a thin line of betrayal against her son for the love of Darius. Will Faith allow her emotions to outweigh her common sense?

In Stores!!!

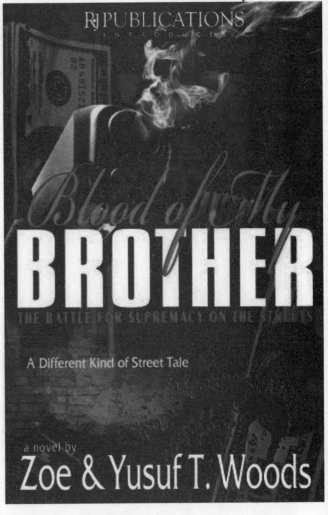

Roc was the man on the streets of Philadelphia, until his younger brother decided it was time to become his own man by wreaking havoc on Roc's crew without any regards for the blood relation they share. Drug, murder, mayhem and the pursuit of happiness can lead to deadly consequences. This story can only be told by a person who has lived it.

In Stores!!!

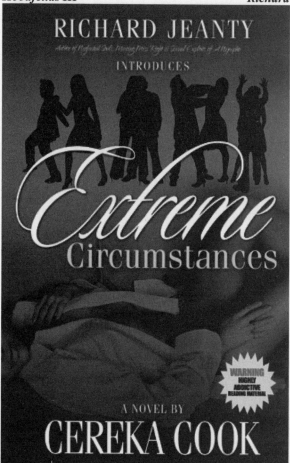

RICHARD JEANTY

Author of Neglected Souls, Mommy Does Know, A Good Catch of A Psycho

INTRODUCES

Extreme
Circumstances

WARNING
HIGHLY
ADDICTIVE
READING MATERIAL

A NOVEL BY
CEREKA COOK

What happens when a devoted woman is betrayed? Come take a ride with Chanel as she takes her boyfriend, Donnell, to circumstances beyond belief after he betrays her trust with his endless infidelities. How long can Chanel's friend, Janai, use her looks to get what she wants from men before it catches up to her? Find out as Janai's gold-digging ways catch up with and she has to face the consequences of her extreme actions.

In Stores!!!

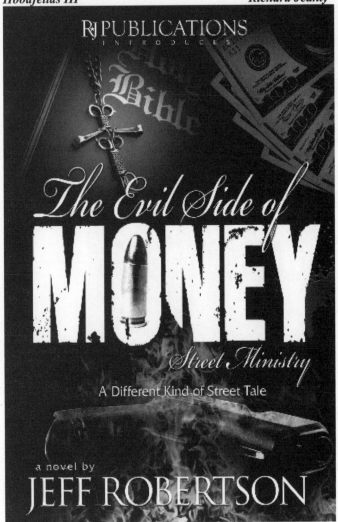

Violence, Intimidation and carnage are the order as Nathan and his brother set out to build the most powerful drug empires in Chicago. However, when God comes knocking, Nathan's conscience starts to surface. Will his haunted criminal past get the best of him?

In Stores!!

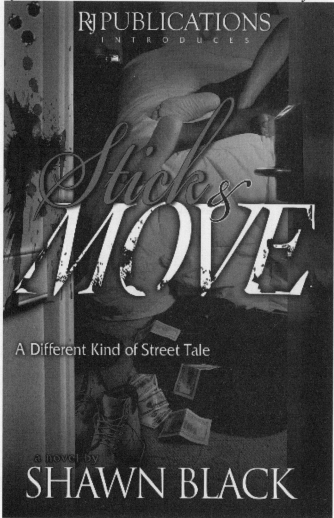

RJ PUBLICATIONS

INTRODUCES

Stick & MOVE

A Different Kind of Street Tale

a novel by

SHAWN BLACK

Yasmina witnessed the brutal murder of her parents at a young age at the hand of a drug dealer. This event stained her mind and upbringing as a result. Will Yamina's life come full circle with her past? Find out as Yasmina's crew, The Platinum Chicks, set out to make a name for themselves on the street.

In stores!!

·

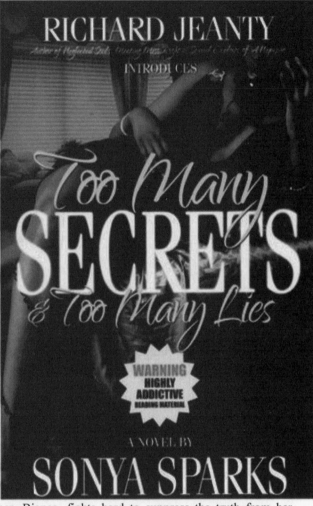

Ashland's mother, Bianca, fights hard to suppress the truth from her daughter because she doesn't want her to marry Jordan, the grandson of an ex-lover she loathes. Ashland soon finds out how cruel and vengeful her mother can be, but what price will Bianca pay for redemption?

In stores!!

Malcolm is a wealthy virgin who decides to conceal his wealth From the world until he meets the right woman. His wealthy best friend, Dexter, hides his wealth from no one. Malcolm struggles to find love in an environment where vanity and materialism are rampant, while Dexter is getting more than enough of his share of women. Malcolm needs develop self-esteem and confidence to meet the right woman and Dexter's confidence is borderline arrogance.

Will bad boys like Dexter continue to take women for a ride?

Or will nice guys like Malcolm continue to finish last?

In Stores!!!

What happens when a woman's devotion to her fiancee is tested weeks before she gets married? What if her fiancee is just hiding behind the veil of ministry to deceive her? Find out as Sean Mitchell takes you on a journey you'll never forget into the lives of Angelica, Titus and Aurelius.

In Stores!!

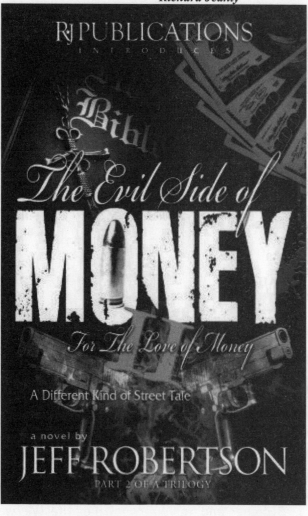

A beautigul woman from Bolivia threatens the existence of the drug empire that Nate and G have built. While Nate is head over heels for her, G can see right through her. As she brings on more conflict between the crew, G sets out to show Nate exactly who she is before she brings about their demise.

In Stores!!!

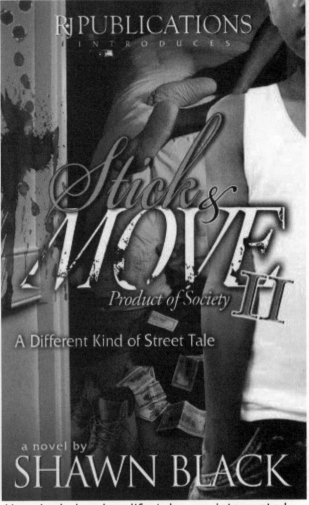

Scorcher and Yasmina's low key lifestyle was interrupted when they were taken down by the Feds, but their daughter, Serosa, was left to be raised by the foster care system. Will Serosa become a product of her environment or will she rise above it all? Her bloodline is undeniable, but will she be able to control it?

In Stores!!

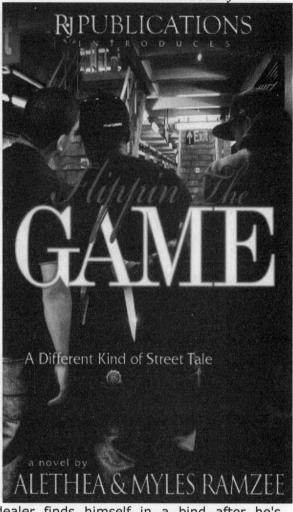

An ex-drug dealer finds himself in a bind after he's caught by the Feds. He has to decide which is more important, his family or his loyalty to the game. As he fights hard to make a decision, those who helped him to the top fear the worse from him. Will he get the chance to tell the govt. whole story, or will someone get to him before he becomes a snitch?

In Stores!!!

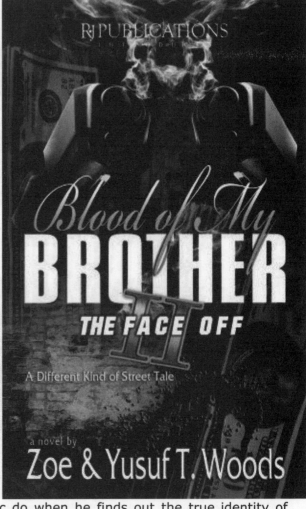

What will Roc do when he finds out the true identity of Solo? Will the blood shed come from his own brother Lil Mac? Will Roc and Solo take their beef to an explosive height on the street? Find out as Zoe and Yusuf bring the second installment to their hot street joint, Blood of My Brother.

In Stores!!!

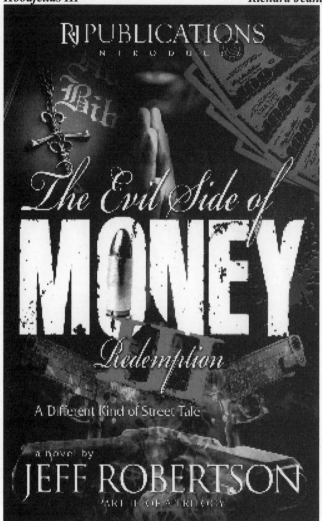

Forced to abandon the drug world for good, Nathan and G attempt to change their lives and move forward, but will their past come back to haunt them? This final installment will leave you speechless.

In Stores!!!

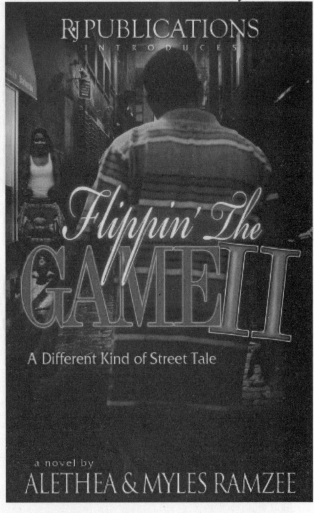

Nafiys Muhammad managed to beat the charges in court and was found innocent as a result. However, his criminal involvement is far from over. While Jerry Class Classon is feeling safe in the witness protection program, his family continues to endure even more pain. There will be many revelations as betrayal, sex scandal, corruption, and murder shape this story. No one will be left unscathed and everyone will pay the price for his/her involvement. Get ready for a rough ride as we revisit the Black Top Crew.

In Stores!!

Dave Richardson is enjoying success as his second book became a New York Times best-seller. He left the life of The Bedroom behind to settle with his family, but an obsessed fan has not had enough of Dave and she will go to great length to get a piece of him. How far will a woman go to get a man that doesn't belong to her?

In Stores!!!

Deon is at the mercy of a ruthless gang that kidnapped him. In a foreign land where he knows nothing about the culture, he has to use his survival instincts and his wit to outsmart his captors. Will the Hoodfellas show up in time to rescue Deon, or will Crazy D take over once again and fight an all out war by himself?

In Stores!!!

The drama continues as Deshun is hunted by Angela who still feels that ex-girlfriend Kayla is still trying to win his heart, though he brutally raped her. Angela will kill anyone who gets in her way, but is DeShun worth all the aggravation?

In Stores!!!

Buck Johnson was forced to make the best out of worst situation. He has witnessed the most cruel events in his life and it is those events who the man that he has become. Was the Johnson family ignorant souls through no fault of their own?

In Stores!!!

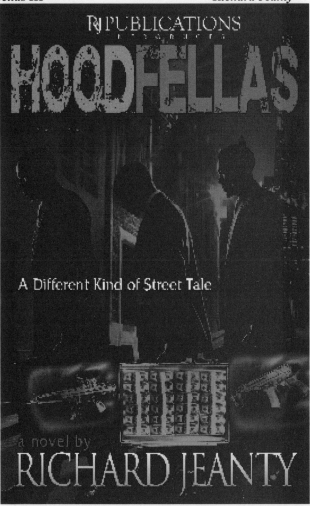

When an Ex-con finds himself destitute and in dire need of the basic necessities after he's released from prison, he turns to what he knows best, crime, but at what cost? Extortion, murder and mayhem drives him back to the top, but will he stay there?

In Stores !!!

What happens when someone falls insanely in love? Stalking is just the beginning.

In Stores!!!

Use this coupon to order by mail

1. Neglected Souls, Richard Jeanty $14.95 Available
2. Neglected No More, Richard Jeanty $14.95Available
3. Ignorant Souls, Richard Jeanty $15.00, Available
4. Sexual Exploits of Nympho, Richard Jeanty $14.95 Available
5. Meeting Ms. Right's Whip Appeal, Richard Jeanty $14.95 Available
6. Me and Mrs. Jones, K.M Thompson $14.95 Available
7. Chasin' Satisfaction, W.S Burkett $14.95 Available
8. Extreme Circumstances, Cereka Cook $14.95 Available
9. The Most Dangerous Gang In America, R. Jeanty $15.00 Available
10. Sexual Exploits of a Nympho II, Richard Jeanty $15.00 Available
11. Sexual Jeopardy, Richard Jeanty $14.95 Available
12. Too Many Secrets, Too Many Lies, Sonya Sparks $15.00 Available
13. Stick And Move, Shawn Black $15.00 Available
14. Evil Side Of Money, Jeff Robertson $15.00 Available
15. Evil Side Of Money II, Jeff Robertson $15.00 Available
16. Evil Side Of Money III, Jeff Robertson $15.00 Available
17. Flippin' The Game, Alethea and M. Ramzee, $15.00 Available
18. Flippin' The Game II, Alethea and M. Ramzee, $15.00 Available
19. Cater To Her, W.S Burkett $15.00 Available
20. Blood of My Brother I, Zoe & Yusuf Woods $15.00 Available
21. Blood of my Brother II, Zoe & Ysuf Woods $15.00 Available
22. Hoodfellas, Richard Jeanty $15.00 available
23. Hoodfellas II, Richard Jeanty, $15.00 03/30/2010
24. Hoodfellas III, Rihard Jeanty 4/15/2011
25. The Bedroom Bandit, Richard Jeanty $15.00 Available
26. Mr. Erotica, Richard Jeanty, $15.00, Sept 2010
27. Stick N Move II, Shawn Black $15.00 Available
28. Stick N Move III, Shawn Black $15.00 Available
29. Miami Noire, W.S. Burkett $15.00 Available
30. Insanely In Love, Cereka Cook $15.00 Available
31. Blood of My Brother III, Zoe & Yusuf Woods Available
32. Mr. Erotica
33. My Partner's Wife
34. Deceived 1/15/2011
35. Going All Out 2/15/2011

Name_____

Address_____

City_____State_____Zip Code_____

　　　　Please send the novels that I have circled above. Shipping and Handling: Free
Total Number of Books_____Total Amount Due_____
　　　　Buy 3 books and get 1 free. This offer is subject to change without notice.
Send institution check or money order (no cash or CODs) to:
RJ Publications
PO Box 300771
Jamaica, NY 11434
For more information please call 718-471-2926, or visit www.rjpublications.com
Please allow 2-3 weeks for delivery.

Use this coupon to order by mail

36. Neglected Souls, Richard Jeanty $14.95 Available
37. Neglected No More, Richard Jeanty $14.95 Available
38. Ignorant Souls, Richard Jeanty $15.00, Available
39. Sexual Exploits of Nympho, Richard Jeanty $14.95 Available
40. Meeting Ms. Right's Whip Appeal, Richard Jeanty $14.95 Available
41. Me and Mrs. Jones, K.M Thompson $14.95 Available
42. Chasin' Satisfaction, W.S Burkett $14.95 Available
43. Extreme Circumstances, Cereka Cook $14.95 Available
44. The Most Dangerous Gang In America, R. Jeanty $15.00 Available
45. Sexual Exploits of a Nympho II, Richard Jeanty $15.00 Available
46. Sexual Jeopardy, Richard Jeanty $14.95 Available
47. Too Many Secrets, Too Many Lies, Sonya Sparks $15.00 Available
48. Stick And Move, Shawn Black $15.00 Available
49. Evil Side Of Money, Jeff Robertson $15.00 Available
50. Evil Side Of Money II, Jeff Robertson $15.00 Available
51. Evil Side Of Money III, Jeff Robertson $15.00 Available
52. Flippin' The Game, Alethea and M. Ramzee, $15.00 Available
53. Flippin' The Game II, Alethea and M. Ramzee, $15.00 Available
54. Cater To Her, W.S Burkett $15.00 Available
55. Blood of My Brother I, Zoe & Yusuf Woods $15.00 Available
56. Blood of my Brother II, Zoe & Ysuf Woods $15.00 Available
57. Hoodfellas, Richard Jeanty $15.00 available
58. Hoodfellas II, Richard Jeanty, $15.00 03/30/2010
59. Hoodfellas III Richard Jeanty 4/15/2011
60. The Bedroom Bandit, Richard Jeanty $15.00 Available
61. Mr. Erotica, Richard Jeanty, $15.00, Sept 2010
62. Stick N Move II, Shawn Black $15.00 Available
63. Stick N Move III, Shawn Black $15.00 Available
64. Miami Noire, W.S. Burkett $15.00 Available
65. Insanely In Love, Cereka Cook $15.00 Available
66. Blood of My Brother III, Zoe & Yusuf Woods Available
67. Mr. Erotica
68. My Partner's Wife
69. Deceived 1/15/2011
70. Going All Out 2/15/2011

Name_____

Address_____

City_____State_____Zip Code_____

        Please send the novels that I have circled above. Shipping and Handling: Free
Total Number of Books_____Total Amount Due_____
        Buy 3 books and get 1 free. This offer is subject to change without notice.
Send institution check or money order (no cash or CODs) to:
RJ Publications
PO Box 300771
Jamaica, NY 11434
For more information please call 718-471-2926, or visit www.rjpublications.com
Please allow 2-3 weeks for delivery.